NIGEL VANE

THE VEILS OF DEATH

Complete and Unabridged

LINFORD
Leicester

First published in Great Britain

First Linford Edition
published 2011

British Library CIP Data

Vane, Nigel.
  The veils of death. - -
  (Linford mystery library)
  1. Detective and mystery stories.
  2. Large type books.
  I. Title II. Series
  823.9′12–dc22

  ISBN 978–1–44480–610–6

Published by
F. A. Thorpe (Publishing)
Anstey, Leicestershire

Set by Words & Graphics Ltd.
Anstey, Leicestershire
Printed and bound in Great Britain by
T. J. International Ltd., Padstow, Cornwall

This book is printed on acid-free paper

THE VEILS OF DEATH

In the same house that his father had committed suicide, Dick Lamont is found brutally stabbed and dying. The last words he utters are odd: 'Caught me . . . never guessed . . . the seventh . . . ' Lamont's sister tells the investigating detective that, just before he died, their father had entrusted her with two silken squares, embroidered with strange black lines; their purpose unknown. Was there any connection between them and the murder in the empty house?

1

The Wrong House

Dr. Leslie Harman pushed his chair back from the dinner table and glanced at his watch. He frowned as he saw that this evening he had been even later than usual in getting home for dinner. The expression in his eyes showed that he had gone short of sleep for some time past, and when he rose to his feet every movement showed his overtired condition.

'Bring my coffee to the study, Simpson,' he ordered the black-garbed butler who hovered round the sideboard, 'and you might take the telephone there as well.'

He crossed the hall wearily, switched on the study lights, and stood for a moment on the threshold as if undecided what to do. A bright fire burned in the grate; the heavy pile of the carpet was soft to his tired feet, and the big saddlebag armchairs spoke to him of pure physical comfort and relaxation after the strain of the day.

He moved over to a table, hesitated again, and picked up a copy of the *Lancet* in its postal wrapper. Taking a cigar from a box on the same table he bit off the end mechanically and sat down in one of the chairs by the fire.

Dr. Harman was a tall, good-looking man of between fifty and sixty, his dark hair rapidly greying at the temples. But for the lines at his eyes and mouth he would have looked younger than his years, for he still possessed the slim figure and upright carriage of youth.

The black-garbed butler entered noise-lessly, drew a small table to the doctor's elbow and placed the coffee on it, then retiring for a moment, he returned with the telephone, which he plugged to a connection in the room.

'Bring it over here, Simpson,' said the doctor. 'Then, if the call is not important I shall not have to get up.'

Simpson did as he ordered, and was about to leave the room when his master spoke again.

'Is the fog clearing off, by any chance?'
The butler shook his head.

'No, sir, worse now than when you came in,' he replied in a soft voice. 'Very thick indeed, sir. One can't even see the nearest street lamp.'

Dr. Harman nodded gloomily.

'It's to be hoped no one wants me to go out this evening,' he said. 'It's difficult enough to find one's way about a strange neighbourhood in the daytime with a fog like this over everything, but in the daytime there are always people to give you some help. Nobody but policemen will be out tonight, I should think.'

Simpson's rather long, sallow face showed his sympathy.

'Very difficult for you, sir,' he murmured. 'If there should be a night call perhaps you would knock me up, sir, and I could come out with you and help you to find your way. When Dr. Lynton went into the nursing home he impressed upon me that I was to give you all the assistance I could.'

A tired smile crossed Dr. Harman's face.

'It's doubtful if you could see further in this pea-soup than I could myself, Simpson,' he said. 'Half the time when I was coming home I couldn't even see the pavement, so I'm afraid your local knowledge wouldn't help much. Thanks all the same. We can only hope there won't be a call.' He paused, and then as the butler turned to go he added: 'Put a decanter and some soda on the table, and then I shan't need to worry you again tonight.'

'Very good, sir,' said Simpson.

As he left the room Harman tore off the wrapper from the *Lancet* and threw it into the fire. Unfolding the journal he scanned the contents while he sipped the coffee, but in a few minutes the paper slipped down on to his knees, and he resigned himself completely to the comfort of his surroundings.

He had taken on the job of *locum tenens* to oblige his friend, Lynton, who had had to go into hospital for an operation, and he was already heartily sick of it. A comfortable private income rendered it unnecessary for him to practise himself, and enabled him to continue the research work that he loved.

He picked up the *Lancet* again, and as he did so he heard the sound of the front doorbell. An expression of annoyance crossed his features and deepened as he heard Simpson admit some visitor. In a few seconds the study door opened and the butler announced:

'Dr. Grey, sir.'

Harman's face cleared as a clean shaven man of about thirty entered the room, and he rose from his chair to greet the newcomer.

'Come in, Grey,' he welcomed heartily. 'Try that chair beside the fire. I've been meaning to ring you up ever since I came last week, but I haven't had a minute. This 'flu epidemic has kept me on the run.'

Robert Grey nodded understandingly as he moved towards the fire and extended his hands towards the blaze.

'I'd have looked you up before,' he said, 'but it was only this morning I heard you were doing *locum tenens* for old Lynton.'

'And a nice time I've had,' grunted Dr. Harman. 'I haven't had two hours' consecutive sleep for the last three days.'

Grey nodded again.

'Yes, I know,' he said. 'It's been pretty much the same with me. Everybody in the district seems to have gone down with this infernal 'flu.'

Dr. Harman made a gesture towards the decanter of whisky on the table.

'Help yourself,' he invited, 'and let's forget there are such things as patients on a miserable night like this.'

Grey accepted the offer at once, poured out a half tumblerful of the whisky, and, splashing in a very little soda, drank it off at a gulp with evident satisfaction. Putting down the tumbler he went back to the fire and sat down in the chair opposite Harman.

'It's a beastly night,' he remarked. 'If I didn't know this end of Sydenham like the palm of my hand I'd have lost my way coming here. It's the thickest fog I've seen for some time.'

'I don't know the neighbourhood at all,' replied Harman. 'Where do you hang out, far from here?'

'A goodish way.' Grey helped himself to a cigarette from his case. 'Lexham Grove, at the foot of West Hill. I had to pass near here on business, so I thought I'd drop in and have a chat.'

'And remarkably welcome you are,' said the other heartily. 'I haven't spoken to a soul that I know ever since I came here. Barring yourself, I don't know anybody in this part of the world.'

'And the last time we met was six months ago,' Grey reminded him. 'At the Slessinger Hospital. Do you remember?'

Harman nodded.

'How are things going with you?' he asked, with the privilege of an old friend. 'You had a fairly lean time after you got your degree, didn't you?'

'Yes, but I'm doing quite well now,' replied Grey, blowing out a cloud of smoke. 'An uncle of mine died three years ago and left me a small legacy. I bought this practice and I've worked it up to quite a profitable concern.'

'You always had the right kind of bedside manner,' chuckled Dr. Harman.

'That sympathetic way of yours ought to appeal to the average patient — especially women.'

Before the other could reply the telephone bell shrilled, and, with a stifled malediction Dr. Harman picked up the instrument.

'Dr. Harman speaking,' he said, and then, as the message came through his face darkened. 'Very well, I'll be round to see her shortly,' he said. 'The address is twenty-six Elm Tree Avenue, you say? Yes, I'll come as soon as I can.'

He put down the telephone and turned to his guest.

'I'm afraid I've got to go out,' he said disgustedly.

Grey looked up.

'What's the trouble?' he enquired. 'Anything serious?'

'I don't know; possibly a false alarm,' replied Harman. 'One of the maids is sick, with a high temperature, and the other maid's a bit worried because all the family are out, and she doesn't know what to do with the invalid. I'll have to go, though how I'm going to find the

8

infernal place in this fog I don't know. Where is Elm Tree Avenue?'

'About a mile and a half away,' said Grey, and reflected for a moment before he added: 'Tell you what, I've got my car at the door. I'll pilot you there. I'll manage it better than you could on a night like this. You can drive behind me and keep your eye on my tail light. I expect you can find your way home all right. It's easier. All you've got to do is to find your way to the main street and stick to it.'

Dr. Harman made no attempt to hide his relief at this solution to his difficulties.

'It's awfully good of you, Grey,' he said gratefully, and glancing ruefully at the warm comfortable room, went over to the window to examine the night.

'Thicker than ever,' he reported. 'You'll have to crawl.'

In a few minutes he had exchanged his slippers for his shoes, warned Simpson to attend to the telephone in his absence and got his car out of the garage at the side of the house. Meanwhile Dr. Grey had started his own engine and was already in his car awaiting him.

'Hoot like blazes the moment you lose sight of me,' he recommended. 'If I hear your hooter I'll stop and hoot back. That should keep us in touch if you should lose sight of my tail-lamp.'

He let in the clutch and started slowly down the road, Dr. Harman falling in behind. The fog was denser than ever, and the headlights of the cars merely illuminated its wreaths without piercing them. As soon as his car had started Harman felt that he had lost touch with the world except for that tail-light ahead of him, and the few square feet of roadway in front of his eyes. The kerb of the pavement had vanished and no lights from the houses lining the road showed through the mist. From time to time the pale splash of a street lamp gleamed high in the air without shedding any light on the ground.

Once the red eye of the guiding tail-lamp almost disappeared from view, and after that he kept closer to the leading car; shifted his foot from the accelerator to the brake and drove on the hand throttle. His eyes began to smart with the sting of the fog, and his throat was rasped as he drew his breath. Even inside the saloon the air had a lungcatching tang, and he could see shadows in it thrown by the nimbus of the headlights in the fog.

Almost from the start he had lost his bearings, and now he pinned his whole attention to Grey's tail-lamp. Once or twice he caught sight of tram-lines beside his wheels and knew they were in the main thoroughfare, but this only gave him the vaguest information regarding their position. The sound deadening quality of the fog completed the sense of isolation. Except for the faint beat of his own engine he seemed to be in a dead and silent world.

Suddenly the sound of Grey's hooter surprised him, and he had to jam on his brake to avoid colliding with the car in front of him. A shadowy figure almost unrecognisable as human moved past him to the rear, and was lost in the fog. Then once more the dim red light ahead moved forward and he followed.

At last Grey's car slid softly alongside a pavement and came slowly to a halt. Dr. Harman pulled up and waited until his guide got down from his seat and came back to him.

'We're just at the turn into Elm Tree Avenue,' announced Grey.

Harman expressed his appreciation.

'That's a pretty good piece of navigation,' he said admiringly. 'You didn't hesitate once.'

'I've a fairly good head for locality,' he said carelessly. 'I think you're all right now. The numbering starts from this side and the even numbers are on the left hand side. The houses are big villas with big gardens, and they all have motor entrances, so if you keep close to the pavement you'll be able to see the break in the kerb and count 'em.'

'Thanks. I doubt if I'd have got here without you, Grey,' said Harman gratefully.

'Glad to have been of help,' retorted Grey. 'Well, I'll be getting along now. See you again soon. Good night. Hope you get home all right.'

He nodded and strode off to his car, and presently Dr. Harman saw the red star, and his contact with the real world, slip away from him and vanish in the fog. When it had gone he let in his clutch again and began to grope his way laboriously along the pavement edge into Elm Tree Avenue.

The fog seemed, if anything, thicker here, and he had the greatest difficulty in detecting even the breaks at the edge of the pavement that indicated the house gates. The walls and the gates themselves were completely invisible behind the curtain of acrid vapour.

He counted seventeen entrances, and was well on the way to the next when suddenly the roar of a horn made him lift his eyes and look ahead. Two golden discs blazed upon him, and only a wild wrench at the wheel saved a collision as the car swept past on the wrong side of the road.

Dr. Harman muttered an imprecation.

'That fellow ought to be hanged!' he grumbled to himself.

In his swerve he had lost touch with the pavement, and now he crept back to the left, steering in gently for fear of grazing his tyres on the kerb. Then he began counting the gates once more.

'Eight — nine — ten — eleven — twelve. It's the next one.'

He passed the next gate and drew up just beyond it. Then, reflecting that it was hardly safe to leave a car on the street on a night like this, he got down from the driving seat and went across the pavement to open the gate of the short drive leading up to the house. The gate was already open, however, and he was about to return to his car when a thought struck him, and he lit a match to examine the pillar.

'No number, of course,' he muttered in annoyance. 'Anyhow, this must be the place.'

Returning to his car, he backed it past the gate and then drove in and up the carriage way. Just in time, as he came near the front door, the lights of a standing car warned him, and he pulled up short.

Shutting off his engine, he got out and approached the house. He glanced into the standing car as he passed and saw that it was empty. There was no light either in the porch of the house or behind the frosted glass of the front door. Dr. Harman ascended the three steps and was about to press the bell when, to his surprise, he saw that the front door was open about six inches. Ringing the bell he waited, but nothing happened. Nobody came. Getting impatient he rang again, keeping his finger on the button. Several seconds passed, but no sound broke the stillness.

'There's something queer here,' he thought. 'Why the devil don't they answer the bell.'

Thinking perhaps that the maid had gone up to her friend and left the door open for him, he stepped on to — bare boards!

He called and the booming echo of his voice came back to him, confirming the suspicion that the bare boards had suggested. The house was empty!

'Confound it,' he muttered angrily. 'I've made a mistake in this infernal fog and come to the wrong house.'

And then he remembered the car he had run into. What was a car doing outside the door of an empty house? He frowned and then shrugged his shoulders. Well, it was none of his business, anyway. He was dead tired. The best he could do would be to try and find the right house. He turned to leave the hall and already had his hand on the door when he heard a sound that brought him to a stop with a jerk.

It was a noise between a muffled cough and a groan, and came from somewhere on his left.

He stood stock still, listening intently, and felt a slight creeping of the hair on his neck. Again he heard that soft, sighing sound, and taking his matches from his pocket, he struck one and looked about him. On his left was a partly closed door. It must have been from behind this that the sound came. He went towards it and pushed it open. As he did so a draught blew out his match and he had to light another one.

In the feeble glimmer he saw that he was looking into a bare room.

He stared at the floor, and the match almost dropped from his fingers.

'Good Heavens!' he ejaculated, and stepping forward he dropped on one knee beside the sprawling figure. It was a man, and his breath was coming in great panting gulps, as he clutched with crimson-stained fingers at his side.

The glazed eyes glared up at Dr. Harman, and the lips moved.

' . . . caught me . . . ' came the choking whisper between the rapid panting breaths. 'Never guessed . . . the seventh . . . '

A spasm contracted his features, and as the match burned down to the doctor's fingers and went out there was a faint gurgling sound, and the breathing ceased.

2

A Cry in The Fog

Kneeling there in the darkness with what he felt sure was a dead man, Dr. Harman suddenly experienced a feeling of fear for the first time in his life.

The empty house, the fog outside, the silence, all combined to add to the terror of that moment when the stertorous breathing stopped and the match went out. It was only for a second that that unusual sensation — as of ice-cold fingers running down his spine — took possession of him. The next he had shaken off his momentary dread, and his methodical brain was working again normally.

Something would have to be done, of course, and done at once. The first thing was to find out definitely whether the man, whoever he was, was beyond medical help. There might be yet a spark of life.

Light was the first essential: he could do nothing in that stygian blackness. Rising to his feet he hurried out to his car. In the pocket on the door beside the wheel he always kept a powerful electric handlamp and with this he returned to the room. Switching it on he placed it on the floor, and, turning it so that its beams flooded the motionless figure, he began a quick examination.

He discovered no sign of life — not the slightest trace of a flutter of the heart or breathing. The man was undoubtedly dead — had died after uttering those disjointed words — and the cause of death was not far to seek. In the centre of the sinister stain that spread over the light tweed overcoat was a clean incision, and when Harman had loosened the clothing he found a deep wound in the left side that corresponded with the cut in the cloth.

The man had been stabbed! This was murder!

The ominous word echoed in his brain, and he straightened up and stood looking at the body. He must inform the police at once. The sooner this affair was off his shoulders the better. But it suddenly flashed across his mind that they might even be suspicious of himself. The mental picture of a methodical and possibly slow-witted police officer questioning him, and perhaps wishing to detain him until the affair was cleared up, formed before his mind. That would be intolerable. His previous weariness, accentuated by the strain of his drive through the fog and the excitement of his discovery, descended upon him in full strength.

He had quite enough to do without becoming involved in a murder case. He stood irresolute, the temptation to go quietly away and let someone else make the gruesome discovery strong upon him; and then the rigour of his training overcame his desire, and he shrugged his shoulders. Of course he would have to inform the police. It was his duty. He pulled out his notebook and jotted the last words of the dying man, noted the time, and slipped the book back in his pocket.

He must have made the mistake in the house when he had swerved to avoid the car that had swept down upon him out of the fog — missed one of the entrance gates before he got back to the pavement. If that was so, then the house he should have gone to was next door. He could phone from there to the police station. The sooner the police were on the premises the better.

Dr. Harman decided to act upon this mental suggestion. Picking up the electric hand lamp he took a last glance at the body and went to the door. It occurred to him as he passed out of the room of death that it would be as well to take precautions that nothing could be disturbed during his absence, and felt to see if there was a key. There was one on the outside, and pulling the door shut he turned the key and put it in his pocket. At the front door he slipped up the catch of the Yale lock so that there was no chance of it fastening, and then went down the steps and out into the fog once more.

The box hedge edging to the drive gave him sufficient guidance through the blinding mist to lead him to the gate, and by following the garden wall thereafter he had little difficulty in making his way to the entrance to what he felt certain must be number twenty-six.

There was no number on the gate pillar here, either, but he groped his way up the drive until the light over the front door shone faintly through the fog. His surmise as to its being the house he sought, however, was confirmed by the figures on the fanlight.

'Why the deuce can't they put them on the gateposts as well,' he muttered irritably, as he climbed the steps and pressed the bell button.

This time he was not kept waiting, for almost at once the door opened, and a middle-aged woman, apparently a cook, peered nervously out at his figure framed in the fog.

'Is that Dr. Harman?' she asked, and then, as he nodded assent, she broke into a torrent of tremulous explanation. 'I thought you were never coming, Doctor. Come in, please. I think Mary's really ill. She's all flushed and her skin's — '

'We'll see about it,' said Dr. Harman reassuringly. 'But first of all I want to ring up about another patient. Where is your 'phone?'

The woman seemed rather put out that he did not go straight at once to see Mary, but she led the way without a word to the room where the telephone was. Harman paused before picking up the receiver, trying to think of an excuse to get the woman out of the way.

'Will you go and put on a kettle of water,' he said. 'I shall probably want some boiling water when I examine the patient.'

The woman went off towards the kitchen, and, closing the door, Harman went quickly to the telephone.

He got through to the police station, briefly related his discovery in the empty house, and had the satisfaction of hearing the sergeant, who answered, promise to be along as soon as possible. He also stipulated that Dr. Harman should remain until the police arrived.

Having attended to this matter the doctor went back to the hall.

The cook was returning from the kitchen.

'The water will be ready in a minute or

two,' she announced. 'Will you want it before you see Mary, or shall I bring it up to you?'

'I may not want it at all,' said Harman. 'Show me the way, please.'

She led him up the stairs to the patient's room, and watched while he made his examination.

'She's got influenza rather badly I'm afraid,' was his verdict. 'Nothing dangerous at present, but we ought to get this temperature down.' He outlined the treatment the girl was to be given, and promised to send some medicine round first thing in the morning, and then as he descended the stairs he asked casually.

'Who occupies the house next door?'

'Mr. Barnwell,' answered the woman.

'That would be number — ' He paused.

'Number twenty-four, sir,' she answered. 'Number twenty-eight is empty, and has been for nearly a year.'

He stopped in the hall and looked round him as the woman raised her hand to unlatch the front door.

'I'm surprised that houses like these

should remain vacant long,' he remarked conversationally. 'I suppose number twenty-eight is the same as this?'

'Yes, sir.' The woman's expression altered, and a curious look came into her eyes. 'But after what happened there it's no wonder they can't let it. It's not altogether pleasant 'aving to live next door.'

Dr. Harman raised his eyebrows.

'Oh, what happened?' he enquired with just the right amount of curiosity.

'Mr. Lamont committed suicide,' said the cook, lowering her voice. 'Hanged himself from the hook behind his bedroom door. It was in all the papers,' she added with a slight touch of pride as though living in such close proximity had endowed her with a partial responsibility for this fact.

'Oh, I see. H'm! Well, of course, that would make it difficult to let,' said Dr. Harman, and after further impressing on her his instructions regarding the treatment of the maid Mary, he took his leave.

His mind was full of what he had just learnt as he crept down the drive and groped his way back to number twenty-eight. Strange that two such fatalities should have happened in the same house. A suicide and a murder with an interval of twelve months separating them. Merely a coincidence, of course, but still strange for all that. Some houses seemed marked out and destined for deeds of violence. He could call to mind a dozen similar cases. It rather bore out the spiritualists' theory that violent thoughts left thought forms behind them that drew others of a like nature. Dr. Harman was too practical to fully believe in these things himself, but still, it was certainly peculiar.

He reached the standing car that had been outside the door of the empty house and paused, suppressing a strong inclination to look inside. He had better not touch anything until the police arrived — might get into trouble if he did, but he could not help wondering whether the car had belonged to the dead man or the murderer.

He went past it and pushed open the front door. The house was as still and silent as when he left it. Leaving the front door open he went to the inside door of the room in which the body lay, and taking the key from his pocket unlocked it. Switching on the hand lamp again he made a leisurely inspection. It was a very large room and had, by the appearance of the paper on the walls, been the drawing room, but there was nothing in it to attract his attention except the dust and that motionless figure on the floor — no sign of the weapon with which the murder had been committed.

He came back to the body and looked down at the dead face. It was that of a fairly young man. Dr. Harman judged his age to have been somewhere in the region of thirty-six. Rather good looking, too, he must have been, with brown hair slightly wavy and tinged with grey at the temples.

He began to speculate as to the reason why he had been killed, and those last strange words. What had the man been trying to say?

'Caught me — never guessed — the seventh — '

What was the meaning of that last word? Did it refer to a date? Certainly not to a current one, for this was the nine-teenth, and if not to a date — to what?

His train of thought was suddenly interrupted by the sound of feet at the front door, and he went out into the bare hall.

Three men were grouped in the doorway, and as he turned the light of the electric lamp on them one of them advanced into the hall.

'Are you Dr. Harman?' he asked gruffly, and Harman saw that he was a thick set man with a little stubby shapeless moustache.

He nodded, and the other continued,

'I'm Inspector Davidson. We got your message at the station and hurried here as quickly as we could, and it was a difficult business with this confounded fog about. You say a man has been killed?'

'Yes,' answered Harman. 'The body's in there.' He indicated the room on the left.

'I've brought the Divisional surgeon with me,' said the Inspector, and turned towards the other two men who had accompanied him and were standing just within the doorway. 'You'd better come along, Doctor, and get your examination over before we do anything else.'

Dr. Harman's eyes travelled to the two men who had come with the Inspector, and he saw that one was a small, thin, rather insignificant little man with horn-rimmed glasses, who carried a black bag. He concluded, since he had made a step forward when Davidson spoke, that this was the Divisional surgeon. The other man was more worthy of attention. He was tall and slim, but with a slimness that gave promise of concealed strength. His face was long and narrow, with firm, well-shaped lips, and a square jaw, and even the brim of the soft hat he wore failed to conceal the keenness of his grey eyes. Even as the little doctor stepped forward, this tall man spoke, and his voice, quiet though it was, held a quality of authority.

'One moment, Inspector,' he interposed. 'Before the Divisional surgeon examines the body I should like to have a glance at the room.'

Inspector Davidson replied with alacrity. Obviously, thought Harman, he

29

regarded this personage with a certain amount of awe.

'Of course, Mr. Quest,' he said. 'By all means. It was exceedingly kind of you to come along on a night like this.'

The tall, lean-faced man smiled.

'You must remember,' he said, 'that I take a certain amount of interest in these things. Perhaps Dr. Harman would lend me his lamp for a moment or two?'

'With pleasure,' said Harman, and handed it over.

The other thanked him and went over to the open door. Standing just inside the threshold he played the light about the room, mostly directing his attention to the floor.

'Did you move about much, Dr. Harman?' he asked.

'I'm afraid I did,' answered the doctor. 'Why?'

'There is nearly a quarter of an inch of dust on this floor,' was the reply, 'and it should have left a very valuable trace of the murderer's footprints. However, we can still pick them out, no doubt, since we shall be able to distinguish yours and the murdered man's quite easily, as we have the originals to help us.' He turned to Inspector Davidson. 'I think it would be as well to do that at once before the traces become even more confused by our own footprints.'

The Inspector agreed and the tall man advanced towards the body, walking on tiptoe and taking a circuitous route. Kneeling down he peered at the dead man's feet.

'There will be no difficulty in recognising his impression,' he announced. 'There is a triangular piece of leather missing from the sole of his right shoe. Dr. Harman, I notice, is wearing rather broad, square-toed shoes, so any other marks there may be can, I think, be taken for those of the murderer.'

He moved round the body, gazing closely at the floor, and almost at once he stopped.

'Here we are,' he said. 'An excellent impression of a rather long, narrow pointed shoe.' His keen grey eyes darted from side to side. 'It looks to me,' he continued, 'as though the murderer and his victim had spent some time talking before he actually committed the crime. The murderer getting more and more excited, until he lost his temper and struck the fatal blow.'

'How do you make that out, Mr. Quest?' asked Inspector Davidson interestedly.

'Because there are signs that he walked up and down on this side of the room several times,' answered Philip Quest, 'while the victim stood still — there are no signs of his footmarks. The murderer's stride, too, varies in length, so I conclude that he was under the influence of some kind of excitement — probably anger.' He straightened up. 'There's nothing more to be learned from those marks,' he said. 'The Divisional surgeon can make his examination now. These prints in the dust should be photographed.'

Dr. Harman watched while the little man made his examination of the body, and in spite of his extreme fatigue he began to feel interested.

So the tall, thin man was the famous Philip Quest whom he had heard so much about. Well, it would be an experience to see how he handled the case. The doctor was not long and his report coincided with Harman's own opinion.

'He was stabbed with a narrow-bladed instrument that pierced the left lung and one of the more important blood vessels,' he announced. 'He must have bled to death — there's probably a considerable amount of internal hæmorrhage, but to what extent I can't tell until after the post mortem.'

'The next thing,' said Inspector Davidson, 'is to try and establish his identity. Perhaps there'll be something — '

He broke off, his sentence trailing away in a gasp. Close at hand and muffled by the fog came a long, terror-laden scream! It rose to a high pitched wail, and then suddenly, like the abrupt silencing of a wireless loudspeaker when the current is shut off, it stopped.

'What in Heaven's name was that?' exclaimed the Inspector, his face a little paler than usual.

'Whatever it was, it wasn't far away,' snapped Philip Quest, and jerking open the door, darted out into the hall!

3

The Girl in The Green Coat

By the time the others had recovered from the first shock of that horrible scream and joined him, Philip Quest was standing at the top of the steps peering out into the fog.

The lights of the two standing cars made four blobs of hazy yellow white in the thick vapour, but that was all — no other sight or sound greeted their straining ears.

'Whoever it was who screamed,' said the detective, 'was somewhere close at hand. We'd better separate and search the drive as best we can.'

He hurried down the steps and disappeared into the mist, fading away to invisibility before he had gone two yards. Inspector Davidson and Dr. Harman followed, the police surgeon, after a moment's hesitation, bringing up the rear.

Harman took the right hand side of the drive and the Inspector the left, and they moved cautiously forward, bent almost double so that they could see the ground at their feet. They were completely cut off from all sight of each other, and except for the vague sound of movement that accompanied their progress each might have been alone.

Dr. Harman looked from right to left as he covered the ground foot by foot. That shrill cry of fear had come from a woman — of that he felt sure, and most equally sure was he that it must have emanated from the street. No woman would be likely to wander about the drive of an empty house in such weather as this. Yet it had, by some strange illusion, seemed nearer than the street.

He heard Quest calling from somewhere.

'Come here quickly,' shouted the detective.

Close at hand the Inspector's voice answered, and Harman almost cannoned into him as his broad form loomed suddenly out of the fog.

They came upon Quest about four yards from the gate, and as they drew close saw that he was bending over a dark heap that lay crumpled up on the gravel of the drive.

'This is a job for you, Doctor,' he said. 'I think she's fainted.'

Harman stooped and saw that the dark heap was the figure of a slim girl, clad in a fur-trimmed bottle green coat, with a small close fitting hat of the same colour. Her eyes were closed and her red lips showed up in startling contrast to her dead-white face. She was breathing irregularly and stertorously, and one little gloved hand lay tightly clenched across her breast.

'We'd better get into the house,' he suggested. 'She appears to have had a pretty bad shock of some kind.'

'Yes,' agreed Quest. 'Will you help me to carry her, Inspector?'

Davidson nodded, and between them they managed to carry the unconscious girl back to the house.

'We'd better not take her in there,' said the detective, as the Inspector was heading towards the room in which the body of the murdered man lay. 'See if one of the other rooms is unlocked.'

There was a door on the opposite side of the hall, and Dr. Harman tried the handle. It was not locked, and after some little difficulty he succeeded in turning it. He held open the door while Quest and the Inspector passed in with their burden.

'If you can hold her for a moment,' said the detective, 'I'll take off my coat and we can lay her on that.'

Davidson swung her up in his powerful arms like a child, and Quest divested himself of his heavy overcoat and spread it on the dirty floor. As soon as the girl had been laid down Dr. Harman set to work to try and restore her to consciousness.

'This may help,' said the detective, and took a flask of brandy from his hip pocket. 'It will be interesting to hear what she was doing in the drive and the cause of her fright.'

They watched while Harman forced a few drops of the spirit between her tightly-compressed lips. She coughed and

37

choked as the brandy trickled down her throat, and then, after one or two convulsive movements opened her eyes.

She stared fearfully up at Harman, and her lips moved.

'Don't!' she whispered. 'Oh, please don't!'

The faint husky voice died to a sob, and Quest stepped forward.

'There is nothing for you to be frightened about,' he said gently. 'You fainted and we found you by the gate. You're quite safe.'

His softly-spoken words seemed to reassure her, and she looked from one to the other while the terror faded from her staring eyes.

'I fainted at the gate!' she repeated, and then as memory supplied the blank: 'Yes — I remember, I was coming up the drive when I ran right into him — '

The look of fear came back into her eyes and she broke off.

'Into whom?' asked Quest.

'A man,' she replied. 'I don't know who he was, but he was going towards the house.' Her voice was growing stronger, and she struggled up to a sitting position, assisted by Dr. Harman's arm. 'I thought it was Dick and — and spoke to him, but he turned on me and gripped me by the throat. I screamed and that's all I remember.'

The Inspector glanced at Quest.

'And who is Dick?' questioned the detective.

'My brother,' answered the girl, and then, looking round the bare, empty room she suddenly shuddered. 'Why have you brought me here? Oh, let me go!'

She tried to struggle to her feet, but Dr. Harman gently pushed her back on Quest's coat.

'You're not in a fit condition to move yet,' he said. 'As to why we brought you here — it was the only place to take you. We couldn't leave you out in the fog.'

'But how did you get in?' she questioned. 'Did Dick let you in?' and then with sudden suspicion. 'Who are you?'

'I'm a doctor,' replied Harman. 'This is a police officer, and — ' He was going to introduce Quest, but at the words police officer she gave a little cry, and the fear returned to her eyes with double intensity.

'A police officer,' she whispered. 'What are the police doing here?'

'There has been rather a serious crime committed here this evening, miss,' said the Inspector. 'And — '

'A crime!' Again she broke in. 'What has happened? Tell me what has happened!'

It was useless to try and keep the facts from her, and anyway, sooner or later she would have to know.

'A man has been stabbed,' said Philip Quest. 'We believe that it was — murder!'

She drew her breath in suddenly with a short, gasping intake as the ominous word left his lips.

'Who — who was killed?' she whispered.

'We don't know yet,' answered the detective. 'We were going to make a second search of the body when you screamed.'

'But what's he like?' her voice rose shrilly and echoed round the bare walls.

'Tell me what he's like!'

Quest described the dead man's appearance as briefly as possible, but he had scarcely got half way through his description when she interrupted him with a cry.

'Oh, Heavens, it's Dick!' she exclaimed wildly. 'It's Dick! What did he want to come here for?' She broke into a violent fit of sobbing.

Dr. Harman did his best to soothe her, and presently she quietened down sufficiently to speak.

'Let me see him,' she demanded huskily. 'Let me see him — there may be some mistake!'

'Do you feel strong enough?' began the detective, but she was on her feet before he could complete the sentence.

'Yes, yes,' she cried. 'I must know!'

Seeing that it would do her more harm to refuse, and realising that a reliable identification of the murdered man was essential, Philip Quest raised no further objections, but taking her by the arm led her across the passage and into the opposite room.

Dr. Harman, holding the electric lamp,

accompanied them, and turned its white rays on the silent figure that occupied the centre of the floor.

The girl stooped and peered down at the upturned face.

'Yes, that's Dick,' she said softly, in a curiously flat, toneless voice. 'That's Dick.'

She swayed, and Harman thought that she was going to faint again, but she recovered.

'Let's go back to the other room,' suggested Quest, and she nodded.

When they had crossed the dark hall and were once more in the opposite room the detective closed the door.

'I hate having to worry you at such a time,' he said, 'but there are several questions I should like to ask you, and which it is essential should be answered at once if we hope to catch the person responsible for the death of your brother. Every second that passes makes our task more difficult.'

The shock seemed to have numbed her, for she looked quite calm and collected as she replied.

'Yes, I quite realise that. I will do all I can to help you.'

'Then in the first place, what is your name?' asked the detective.

'Celia Lamont,' she answered, and as he heard the name Dr. Harman started.

The name of the original tenant of that empty house who had hanged himself from the hook behind his bedroom door. And now another member of the family had passed into eternity in that gloomy building. Surely it was more than coincidence? Surely the house possessed some evil influence!

'And your brother's name?' said Philip Quest, breaking in on the doctor's thoughts.

'The same,' she replied dully. 'I am not married.'

'Will you tell me, Miss Lamont,' the detective continued, 'what your brother was doing here on a night like this?'

'I would if I could,' she said shaking her head, 'but I don't know.'

'Then perhaps you can tell me why you came here?' said Quest.

'I came to look for Dick,' she answered.

'So you knew he was coming here, although you didn't know why,' said the detective.

'Yes, I knew he was coming here,' she said.

'Did he tell you?'

Again she shook her head.

'No, the maid told me,' she replied. 'I had been to a friend's house to borrow a book, and I stayed there talking for about an hour. When I got home I found that Dick had gone out. I was rather surprised as he was rather keen on listening to the wireless programme this evening. I asked Doris — that's the maid — if she knew where he had gone, and she said that a gentleman had called about half an hour after I had left, and that he and Dick had gone off together.'

'How did the maid know where they had gone?' asked Quest.

'She heard Dick tell the man just before they were leaving that he had an old key that he'd never given up to the agents.'

'But how could she be certain that he was referring to the key of this house?'

'She wasn't,' said the girl, 'but I guessed that was what Dick had meant by the reference to the key. I knew that he had got an old front door key, and that he kept it in the handkerchief drawer in his bedroom with several other keys that he didn't use. I went up to make sure and it was gone.'

'I see,' said Quest. 'And what made you come here in the fog?'

'I was worried,' she answered. 'The whole thing seemed so extraordinary. The man who had called for Dick was a stranger. Doris knows all our friends and she was certain that she had never seen this man before, and it seemed so peculiar that Dick or any one else should want to go to an empty house on a foggy night like this. It was too late for a prospective tenant, and, besides, people don't usually look over a house in a fog. I couldn't understand it at all, and at last I got so uneasy that I came to see if I could find Dick and — and — '

Her voice broke and tears began to flow down her cheeks once more. She choked them back, however, and wiped her eyes with a whispy handkerchief.

'Do you live far from here?' asked Quest.

'No,' she answered. 'Park Road. It's practically the opposite turning after you cross the main road.'

'As soon as we have finished here I will accompany you home,' said the detective. 'It is essential that we should get a description from your maid of this man who called on your brother. I suppose the man who attacked you in the drive was a stranger to you?'

'I didn't see very much of him,' she replied. 'Except that he was tall and rather thin.'

'You wouldn't be able to recognise him again, Miss?' put in the Inspector.

The girl shook her head.

'No, I'm afraid I shouldn't,' she said. 'I never saw his face at all.'

'Pity,' muttered Quest. 'If you had been in a position to identify him it might have saved a lot of trouble.' He frowned. 'You say he was going towards this house,' he continued. 'You are sure he wasn't coming away from it?'

Again she shook her head.

'Quite sure,' she answered. 'He was walking up the drive.'

Philip Quest pursed his lips thoughtfully. Who was this mysterious man who had been coming to that house of death? The murderer returning to the scene of his crime? It was possible but extremely unlikely unless he had a very pressing reason — a reason that was sufficiently powerful to make the risk he ran of secondary consideration. Something, perhaps, that he had, in his panic following the killing, left behind — some evidence that if found would incriminate him. An idea occurred to the detective and he turned once more to the girl.

'Did your brother possess a car?' he asked quickly.

'No,' she replied and looked at him questioningly. 'Why?'

Philip Quest made no reply to her question but addressed his next remark to Harman.

'Dr. Harman,' he said, 'when you first arrived at this house you found a car standing in the drive, I think?'

The doctor nodded.

'Then, since it did not belong to the dead man, Mr. Lamont,' the detective continued, 'it is only reasonable to suppose that it belonged to the man who called for him and accompanied him here. I think, Inspector, it would be as well if we had a look at that car without delay and see if there is anything in it that will identify its owner.'

Inspector Davidson agreed with alacrity, and leaving Harman to look after the girl, followed Quest once more out into the fog. It was thinning slightly, and the car, with its still lighted headlamps, stood as Harman had first seen it, but now more plainly visible. It was an old machine, of a cheap and well known make, and an examination showed that it had been well used. The tyres were worn; scarcely any of the original treads remained, and the panel work was scratched and blistered, showing portions of rusty metal beneath.

'Looks as if it were only fit for the scrap heap, sir,' remarked the Inspector, peering disgustedly at the decrepit vehicle and noting the number — XV6094.

Quest nodded and pulled open one of the doors.

'Let's see if there's anything inside,' he muttered, and leaned forward to gaze into the interior.

It was too dark to see anything until he switched on his torch, and then he saw that the interior was, if anything, more disreputable than the exterior. The cord upholstery was cut and torn, stained and dirty. Quest lifted the cushions of the seats but found nothing, nor was there anything in the pockets attached to the doors.

'There's nothing here to help us, Inspector,' he said disappointedly, and turned his attention to the driver's seat and the dashboard. The seat — like the others — yielded nothing, but in the dashboard was a small compartment for the reception of cigarettes or other oddments, and in this the detective discovered a partly torn piece of paper.

'Found something, sir?' asked the inspector eagerly, as Quest extracted the paper and straightened up.

The detective nodded, and under the rays of his torch, with the Inspector looking over his shoulder, examined his find.

The paper was crumpled and dirty, and on it were two lines of pencilled writing. They ran:

'Lamont has got the key. He lives at number twenty Park Road.'

That was all. The rest, together with a signature — if there had ever been one — was missing.

4

A Fresh Developement

'That doesn't help us much, sir,' said the Inspector disgustedly, and Quest agreed with him. 'I suppose the key referred to is the key to this house,' Davidson went on.

'Apparently,' said the detective. 'Though it seems funny to me that if the object was merely to gain admittance to this place so much trouble should have been taken to get hold of the actual key. In this fog it would have been child's play to effect an entrance.'

'Why should anyone want to get into an empty house?' remarked the Inspector, shaking his head. 'Unless it was for the purpose of committing the murder — '

'I don't think that was the primary reason,' broke in Quest. 'I think there's something very queer behind this crime. For one thing, why should the murderer have abandoned his car? He must have known that directly the fog lifted it would be seen and attract attention to the house. Why did he leave it here — with the lights full on?'

'Perhaps the arrival of Dr. Harman disturbed him,' suggested Davidson.

'That's possible,' assented Quest. 'But even that seems to me unlikely. If he was hiding out here in the fog when the doctor arrived, why didn't he take the opportunity when Harman was in the house to make off in the car?'

'The only other reason I can think of, sir,' said Inspector Davidson, 'is that he thought the car would hamper his escape: I mean the fog, being like it was.'

'Yes, that's a very reasonable suggestion,' said the detective, 'and if it's a true one it leads to a further conclusion.'

'What's that, sir?' asked Davidson.

'That the car was either stolen or hired for the occasion,' replied Quest. 'If it was the murderer's own property he wouldn't have dared take the risk of leaving it. He'd have realised it could be traced through the registration.'

'That's true.' Davidson nodded his

round head. 'Of course, we shall have to put through an enquiry. There's just a chance that the car was abandoned through panic. I've known murderers do sillier things than that.'

'So have I,' said Quest. 'But I don't think you'll find there was any panic in this business. The whole thing strikes me as well ordered and thought out. Let's go back to the house.'

He turned without waiting for the Inspector to reply, and made his way to the gloomy porch. In the room on the left the Divisional Surgeon, Dr. Harman, and the girl were standing where he had left them, and at his approach Harman came forward.

'I should like to get away as soon as possible,' he said. 'I've had a tremendously busy time lately, and I'm dog tired.'

'I don't think there's any need to keep you, Doctor,' said Quest. 'You'll have to make a statement at the station relating how you found the dead man. Inspector Davidson will arrange that.'

'Yes, I suppose I shall,' Harman

nodded shortly. 'I think I ought to tell you that he wasn't dead when I found him.'

Quest looked round quickly. He had been on the point of going over to the girl.

'Wasn't dead?' he repeated enquiringly.

Harman shook his head.

'No,' he replied. 'In fact, he spoke — I made a note of his exact words.'

He took out his notebook and the detective's eyes glinted.

'This is very interesting, Doctor,' he said. 'What did he say?'

'I don't know if you can make anything of it; I couldn't,' confessed Harman. 'He just managed to gasp out: 'Caught me — never guessed — the seventh,' and then he died.'

Philip Quest's long lean fingers went up and curled about his chin. From his chin they strayed up to the side of his face, and his brows met.

'The seventh?' he muttered. 'The seventh — what?'

Harman shrugged his shoulders.

'That's what puzzled me,' he said. 'But that's what he said. He spoke plainly enough for me not to have made a mistake.'

Inspector Davidson appeared before the detective could reply, and with him came the tall, uniformed figure of a policeman. Philip Quest took him aside and repeated what Harman had just told him. The Inspector raised his eyebrows.

'Can't make head or tail of it at the moment, sir,' he said. 'We may find it's important later.'

'I think you will,' said the detective. 'Particularly that reference to the seventh.'

Davidson shot him a quick glance.

'Have you got anything at the back of your mind?' he asked.

Quest smiled and shook his head.

'Not at the moment,' he admitted. 'I'm merely telling you what I think. It's an odd thing to have said, and oddities in a case like this are worth noting, that's all.'

He looked over the Inspector's shoulder at the girl, who, rather pale and tired-looking, was now leaning against the dingy wall as though she found the strain of standing without support too much for her.

'I think we ought to get Miss Lamont home,' he said. 'She's had rather a shock; and besides, we want if possible to get a description of the man who called from the maid.'

'Yes, you're right,' agreed Davidson. 'I'll finish up here and leave the constable in charge, and come along with you.'

He went over to the man who stood by the door and spoke to him in a low voice. When he had finished giving his instructions, Dr. Harman again put forward his request to be allowed to go.

Davidson nodded.

'The ambulance will be here in a few minutes, Doctor,' he said, 'and my sergeant's coming with it. If you will accompany him to the station and make your statement regarding the finding of the body, I shan't have to trouble you again tonight.'

He looked across at the little police surgeon.

'I suppose you'll be waiting for the ambulance, too?' he said.

'Yes, I might as well,' was the brisk reply. 'They can drop me at the station and I can make my report at the same time as Dr. Harman and get it over.'

Inspector Davidson glanced quickly round.

'Then I think, if you're ready, Mr. Quest,' he said, 'we'll go with Miss Lamont.'

The girl, who had been staring at the floor, evidently occupied with her own thoughts, looked up on hearing her name.

Philip Quest crossed to her side.

'Will you come with us?' he said gently.

'Where?' she asked dully.

'Home,' he replied. 'It is necessary that we should question your maid.'

She nodded, and walked towards the door in a listless, lifeless way, like an automaton infused with movement, but totally devoid of all feeling.

'Wait here until I come back, Pinner,' ordered Davidson as he passed the policeman and followed Philip Quest and the girl out into the front garden.

The slight thinning of the fog that they had noticed had increased. It was possible now to see the other side of the road and the houses that lined it. At the kerb stood the little two-seater in which the Inspector and the Divisional Surgeon had come, and into this Davidson packed himself, the detective and the girl.

It took them less than two minutes to reach Park Road, and the girl stopped the car about a hundred yards down on the right hand side.

'This is our house,' she said.

Philip Quest looked at it as he extricated his long form with difficulty from the confines of the little car.

It was not so large as that other house they had so recently left, and here there was no drive. Only a small square of garden separated it from the side walk bordered by a trim hedge. There were no lights in any of the windows or behind the glass fanlight over the front door.

The detective assisted the girl to alight and held open the wooden gate.

'I expect Doris is in bed,' she said as she fumbled in her bag for the key. She opened the front door and preceded Quest and the Inspector into the gloom of the tiny hall.

The detective sniffed as she crossed the threshold. A faint peculiar odour reached his nostrils, like the smell of apples. Celia Lamont reached out her hand and the darkness was dissipated by the soft glow of a shaded lamp.

'If you will go in here — ' she began, and stopped, staring.

Philip Quest frowned. He had already seen the cause of that sudden break in her sentence. The furniture in the hall was not in the neat order it should have been. Rugs were crumpled and askew; an oak chest was open, and its contents tumbled in a heap beside it; a chair lay overturned against the foot of the stairs.

'What's been happening here?' muttered Davidson. 'Looks as though someone had been searching for something.'

Philip Quest's face was grave as he looked about him.

'I hope it's nothing worse,' he said, and following the direction of his eyes, the girl gave a low cry. On the creamy surface of the wall, close by the front door, was a glistening smear.

The detective stepped over and put his finger to it. It was blood, and it was still wet!

5

The Two Veils

Inspector Davidson's breath was drawn in a long hissing gasp.

'It looks as if something pretty bad had been happening here, sir,' he said, going over to Philip Quest's side.

The detective nodded.

'Was your maid alone in the house, Miss Lamont?' he asked.

'Yes,' answered the girl, her eyes wide and frightened. 'We only have one servant. My — my brother and I lived alone — '

'Where does your maid sleep?' Quest continued as she paused. 'Which is her room?'

'At the top of the house,' answered the girl. 'I'll go up and — '

'I'd rather you didn't do anything of the kind,' broke in the detective. 'I think it would be better if you waited here with

Inspector Davidson. I'll go.'

'There are two rooms on the top landing,' she said as he moved towards the staircase. 'Doris' is the one on the right.'

Quest went quickly up the stairs. The house was a three storied one and he had no difficulty in locating the maid's room. The door was wide open, and before he switched on the light he knew that the room was empty. It was small and plainly furnished and from the tumbled appearance of the bed Doris had evidently retired for the night before — What? Something that had disturbed her and brought her down? Some sound that had wakened her from sleep? No, it couldn't have been that. She would scarcely have had time to fall asleep since her mistress had left. But what had happened to her? Quest thought of that ugly patch of crimson on the wall below, and his lips compressed.

He went over to the other door and opened it. There was evidently no globe in the light pendant here, for pressing the switch failed to elicit any responsive flood of light, but he could dimly make out a pile of trunks and boxes. It was a much smaller room than the other, and obviously used as a store room.

He was closing the door when he heard the Inspector's voice calling from the hall. There was an urgent note in it that sent Quest hurrying down the stairs as fast as he could. Davidson was standing in the hall looking up.

'I've found the girl, sir,' he greeted as Quest reached the bottom of the stairs. 'Look here!'

He crossed the hall to an open door on the left. The lights were on and as Quest peered in he saw the huddled form on the big settee that was drawn up by the fireplace.

'She's still alive,' said the Inspector, 'but she's had a nasty crack on the head.'

She lay breathing heavily and irregularly, her eyes closed and her mouth half open. As the detective bent over her he caught another whiff of the apple-like odour.

'Drugged, too,' he muttered. 'She's had a dose of chloroform.'

He examined the wound on her forehead. There was a big bruise and the skin had been broken, which accounted for the blood that matted her hair, but it wasn't serious. Quest slipped a cushion under her head and turned to the Inspector.

'The best thing we can do is to wait until she comes round of her own accord,' he said. 'I shouldn't think it would be long before the drug wears off.'

Davidson nodded.

'It's pretty easy to see what happened, sir,' he said. 'She was brought down by a ring at the door and attacked. That smear of blood in the hall must have been where her head struck the wall as she fell. After that they made sure of keeping her quiet with chloroform.'

'I think you've reconstructed what happened fairly accurately,' agreed the detective. 'The question: what was the reason for it all?'

He looked about the room. It was a comfortably furnished apartment — a combination drawing room sitting room — and it had evidently been subjected to a rigorous search.

A bookcase had been denuded of its contents, which lay about untidily on the floor. The drawers of a cabinet gaped open, and a small bureau writing desk had been thoroughly ransacked.

'Whoever was responsible for the attack on the maid wanted something pretty badly,' the detective continued. 'I wonder if they've treated the entire house the same way?'

'I'll have a look over it, sir,' said Davidson, and went out into the hall, passing Celia Lamont, who was standing just inside the doorway.

When he had gone Philip Quest pushed forward an easy chair and took her gently by the arm.

'Sit down, Miss Lamont,' he said. 'I'm afraid you've had a severe shock tonight, and I must apologise for troubling you any further, but there are some questions which I should like to ask you which are essential.'

'Don't worry about me,' she said in a curiously flat, toneless voice. 'I feel too — too' — she searched for a word

— 'numbed I think is the best description. I haven't fully realised. It's like cutting your finger badly. You don't feel the pain until sometime after. Do you understand?'

'Yes, I think I do,' said Quest, and he did.

The worst time for Celia Lamont was to come when the first shock had worn off, and her doped senses had returned to normality.

'The first thing I want to ask you,' the detective continued after a little pause, 'is this: Have you any idea what the person or persons who came here tonight were looking for?'

She shook her head.

'No,' she replied. 'I haven't the least idea, Mr. Quest.'

'There was nothing of value — no large sum of money or jewellery?' suggested Quest, and again she shook her head.

'No,' she said. 'I have no jewellery and there is very little money. After father's tragic death his affairs were found to be in a very involved state. When everything had been sorted out there was scarcely enough to live on.'

'Your father's tragic death?' repeated the detective quickly. 'What do you mean by that, Miss Lamont?'

The white face raised to his went if anything a shade whiter, but the voice was steady enough as she spoke.

'He — he hanged himself a year ago in that house where Dick was killed tonight!'

Philip Quest felt a sudden thrill of interest run through him. So the murder of Richard Lamont was not the first tragedy that that dismal and deserted house had witnessed! It had seen another. Suicide and murder! Was there any connection?

'I am sorry to have to reopen an unpleasant subject,' he said gently, 'but do you know why your father took his life?'

'No,' she answered, 'we never knew why. He had been worried for a long time before — before it happened, but he never told us why.'

'And you can think of nothing that is likely to throw any light on your brother's death or the reason for a search having been made of this house?' said Quest.

'Nothing,' replied the girl.

'Try and think,' urged the detective. 'Perhaps there is some little incident — something quite trivial — that may be the means of providing us with a clue.'

'I'm afraid there isn't — ' she began, and stopped, her face changing.

'You've thought of something,' said Quest watching her. 'What is it?'

'I don't suppose it has any connection really,' she said. 'Perhaps you'll think it stupid of me to mention it. It's merely something my father gave me a week before he died.'

'Nothing is too stupid to mention in a case of murder,' said the detective gravely. 'It has been my experience that the most trivial things have been the means of leading the way to the truth. Tell me all about this thing your father gave you.'

'It was a small packet,' she said, 'and contained two veils of silken net.'

'Veils?' echoed Philip Quest.

She nodded.

'Yes, very finely worked and about a yard square. I asked father what they were for, but he wouldn't tell me. All he said was that if anything happened to him I was to keep them.'

She took her handbag which lay in her lap, and, opening it, drew from a side pocket in the interior an envelope.

'I'll show you the veils,' she said. 'I have always carried them about with me. Father was very particular about that when he gave them to me.'

She opened the envelope and carefully withdrew the contents, Quest watching her curiously.

There were two squares of silken net of gossamer fineness — so fine that they looked like spiders' webs. Each was delicately embroidered with black silk — a patternless jumble of fine lines — and as the girl shook them out and they almost floated in the slight draught from the door the detective saw that at each corner was a small round hole, a button hole stitched with the same black silken thread. He looked at the fine veils carefully.

'You have no idea what these were for?' he asked.

'No,' she said. 'Father only told me to keep them, and to always keep them by me.'

Philip Quest's brows wrinkled in a puzzled frown. What was the purpose of these silken veils? Was there any connection between them and the crime in the empty house, and was it for these that such a vigorous search had been made in the house in Park Road that night?

6

A Baffling Problem

Celia Lamont watched Philip Quest in silence while he carefully examined the squares of gossamer silk, trying to extract some hidden meaning from them. At first he thought it probable that the design, so skilfully worked in black all over the surface, might supply a reason for their existence, but he soon found that this was not so.

He had for a moment imagined that the curly lines and scrolls might conceivably be twisted into some message, but a short inspection quickly proved that this idea was wrong. They made no sort of sense; indeed, did not even conform to any set pattern. The secret of the veils — if secret there was — was beyond Quest, as he was presently to be forced to admit. And yet, did he but know it, he held in his hand the clue to the whole problem, but it was to be many weeks later that he realised this.

'I can make nothing of these at all, Miss Lamont,' he said at last looking across at the girl. 'So far as I can see they appear to be very ordinary. You have no idea, I suppose, how they came to be in your father's possession originally?'

'I never saw them until the day he handed them to me,' she answered. 'How he got possession of them or what they were for I haven't the least idea.'

'They are of very fine workmanship,' remarked the detective, fingering them softly — 'very fine indeed. And apparently your father considered them of value, or he wouldn't have stipulated that you should always carry them about with you. You say it was a week before the — er — tragedy that he gave you these?'

She nodded.

'Yes. He gave them to me on a Saturday,' she replied. 'On the following Saturday morning we — we found him — ' She stopped abruptly.

'Curious!' Philip Quest's long fingers tapped gently on the back of a chair. 'I don't want to rake up unpleasant memories, Miss Lamont, but I should like to hear more about the circumstances surrounding your father's death.'

She smiled — a rather wan smile that was like a pale wintry sun breaking through a cloudy sky.

'Time has blunted my feelings regarding father's death,' she said. 'Besides, I had to go over the story so many times that to do so again won't make any difference. What is it you want to know?'

'Everything,' answered Quest promptly. 'I have an idea — a hunch is a more explicit word — that that year old tragedy may have a direct bearing on this later crime.'

'I don't see very well how it can,' she said, shaking her head slowly. 'But I'll tell you all I know concerning father's death.'

She wrinkled her brows and considered for a moment, and then she went on quickly and a little jerkily:

'We were living then at the house in Elm Tree Avenue. Dicky, father and myself; mother had been dead for years. Father, who was an engineer, had only been home from abroad for six months. He had been in Africa for nearly two years, at a place close to Johannesburg, superintending some mining operations — I don't know quite what they were — but when he returned he was different somehow.'

She paused, but Quest made no comment. He concluded that it was better to let the girl tell the story in her own way without interruption.

'It would be difficult for me to explain exactly how he was different,' she continued, 'but he was. Both Dicky and I noticed it and talked about it. He was more abrupt, seemed to dislike company of any sort, and spent most of his time locked in his study. When we did come in contact with him, which was seldom, he was just as kind and considerate as ever but — I don't know how to put this, but I will hope you will understand what I mean — he seemed always to be thinking of something else. He would join in the conversation and answer questions, but more or less mechanically, as if he were only giving half his attention to what you were saying and the rest of his mind was elsewhere. Do you know what I mean?'

'Yes,' said the detective. 'Go on!'

'I asked him once,' said the girl, 'if there was anything worrying him, and he was quite cross — so angry that I never attempted to question him again. But although he wouldn't say, it was obvious that there was something troubling him. He would start at the slightest sound, and once, when a tyre burst in the street just outside the house, he nearly fainted.'

'Was he always of a nervous disposition — like that?' asked Quest as she stopped.

Celia shook her head.

'No. That's what made it so noticeable,' she replied. 'Even the servants saw the change in him. We had a cook then as well as Doris.'

'And this change only occurred after his return from Johannesburg. M'm,' murmured the detective thoughtfully.

The girl looked at him quickly.

'You're thinking — as I thought at the time,' she said, 'that something happened in Africa. But you're wrong. Nothing happened there that would account for his strange behaviour.'

'How do you know?' asked Quest in surprise.

'Because after his tragic death I had enquiries made. A great friend of ours' — she flushed slightly, and Quest drew his own conclusions regarding the sex and with whom the friendship had been greatest — 'a great friend of ours was going out to Johannesburg on business, and I asked him to make enquiries. And he said that there was absolutely nothing.'

'Is this friend of yours still abroad?' said the detective.

'No,' she answered. 'He's back now. He has been back for about four months.'

'I should like to see him,' said Quest.

'He lives quite close to here,' she replied. 'On West Hill. His name is James Harding.'

The detective made a note of the name and of the address she gave him.

'Now go on with your story,' he said. 'I must apologise for interrupting.'

She frowned.

'I'm afraid there's very little more to tell,' she confessed. 'Only one queer incident that's worth repeating. It was on the morning that father gave me those' — she nodded towards the veils which Quest had laid on the table — 'we were at breakfast, father, Dicky and I, and father was reading the paper. Suddenly he gave a low cry and went quite white. He recovered himself almost at once, and said that he had had a sudden sharp twinge of toothache. But I knew it wasn't that.'

'What do you think it was?' said Quest.

She hesitated, and then, as though making up her mind, looked him full in the face.

'I thought — and I still think — that it was something he read in the paper,' she answered steadily.

Philip Quest returned the gaze.

'Beyond just thinking that,' he said, 'have you any proof?'

'No, none,' she answered, shaking her head slowly. 'I looked all through the paper later on that day, but I could find nothing to support my idea. But, all the same, I'm certain that it was something in the paper.'

'What was the paper?' asked the detective.

She told him, together with the date, and he decided that at the first opportunity he would consult the file for that particular copy and see if he could find what it was that had caused the elder Mr. Lamont such agitation.

'And this was the week before his — his death?' he said.

She nodded.

'Yes,' she replied. 'Exactly a week. The following week Doris found him. There was a large hook behind the door in his bedroom and he had used this and — and his dressing-gown cord — '

Her voice grew husky and trailed away into silence. There was a little pause.

'And there was no note?' said the detective. 'He left nothing to show why he should have taken his own life?'

'No.' Her voice was clear and steady again. 'He had destroyed all his private papers. The study and the bedroom were in an appalling state. Things were thrown all over the place — '

She stopped and looked round quickly

as a heavy step sounded from the hall and Inspector Davidson came in.

'The whole house has been turned upside down,' he reported. 'Whoever the fellow was and whatever he was looking for, he's made a thorough job of it. Not a square inch has been overlooked.'

'There is, of course, no clue to his identity?' said Quest, and Davidson shook his large head.

'Nothing at all,' he replied. 'The only hope we've got is the girl.'

He jerked his thumb towards the settee.

'When she recovers she may be able to give us a description of her assailant.'

Philip Quest shrugged his shoulders.

'I doubt it,' he replied. 'I don't think this is going to be such an easy business as that, Davidson.'

'I'm rather inclined to agree with you, sir,' said the big inspector. 'Anyhow, we shall soon know. The girl is beginning to recover now.'

Three pairs of eyes turned towards the settee as Doris stirred slightly and gave a little choking moan.

7

Doris Tells Her Story

'Drink this,' ordered Philip Quest, holding the steaming cup of coffee to the shivering girl's lips. 'You'll feel better.'

Doris meekly obeyed, gulping the scalding fluid until she broke into a violent fit of coughing.

After that first movement her recovery had been rapid, and her first conscious reaction had been one of extreme sickness. Quest had ordered coffee hot and strong, and while Davidson had hastily prepared this the detective had set to work to restore the drugged maid to the full use of her senses.

'Feel better now?' he asked kindly, when she had finished coughing, and she nodded, looking at him with streaming eyes.

'All but an 'eadache,' she replied. 'Fair splittin' it is.'

'Take these, Doris,' said Celia, and took from her bag a small box of aspirin tablets.

Doris took them gratefully, washing them down with a further draught of coffee. Her little button of a nose was deep red, and she looked anything but prepossessing as she lay back in a corner of the big settee and gaped tremulously from one to the other.

'Now, Doris,' said Philip Quest, when he had allowed her time to collect her obviously scattered wits, 'I want you to tell us exactly what happened.'

Doris screwed up her small face in a concentrated effort of thought.

'When Miss Celia went out,' she began at last, 'she told me not to wait h'up for 'er, so I locked up the back door and went up to bed. I'd just got undressed and put out the light and settled down comfortable-like when the knocker goes. Bang, bang, bang! it goes, like a postman, but I knew it couldn't be no postman at that time of the night. I thought p'r'aps Miss Celia or Mr. Dick had gone out without their keys, so I made me way down the stairs to the 'all and opens the front door. There was a man on the step and 'e says, speakin' 'usky-like as if 'e'd got a cold: 'Mr. Lamont live 'ere?' 'Yus,' I says, and was just goin' ter tell 'im that everybody was out when 'e leans forward and 'its me over the 'ead with somethin' 'e's got in 'is 'and. That's all I remember until I woke up 'ere.'

She had rattled this off in one breath, without a break or a pause, and now she stopped, panting.

'What was this man like?' asked Philip Quest.

'I couldn't tell yer,' replied Doris. 'I didn't 'ave time ter see.'

'But you must be able to give us some sort of description,' urged the detective. 'Was he short or tall? How was he dressed?'

'He wasn't short or tall,' she answered. 'He was just ordinary, and he had on a dark overcoat and a cap.'

'You didn't see his face, Miss' suggested the Inspector.

'No, I didn't,' said Doris decidedly. ''E 'ad 'is cap pulled right down over 'is eyes.

I couldn't see nothing of what 'e looked like.'

'Tell me,' said Quest. 'Earlier this evening a man called for Mr. Lamont. Was there any resemblance between this man and the man who attacked you?'

Doris shook her head, and winced as the movement set it aching.

'No, they wasn't a bit alike,' she answered. 'The gentleman what come ter see Mr. Dick was tall and thin, and 'ad on a slouch 'at an' a waterproof — '

'Did you see his face?' broke in Davidson quickly.

'Yes, 'course I did,' answered the maid. 'He was a funny-lookin' feller, sort of yeller colour, with a little black moustache and side whiskers — like one of them Spanish fellers yer see on the pitchers.'

'You mean he wasn't English?' said the Inspector.

'That's what I said, didn't I?' snapped Doris.

For some reason or other she appeared to have taken an intense dislike to the stout official.

'Did he speak English?' asked Quest. 'I mean, was there any trace of a foreign accent?'

'He spoke Henglish,' said Doris, 'as well as I do meself.'

'You would be able to recognise this man again, Miss?' said Davidson.

'Oh yes,' replied Doris. 'He's the sort of man you could pick out of a crowd.'

'You have, I suppose, never seen him before?' said Quest. 'I mean, you haven't noticed him while you have been out shopping.'

'No,' snapped Doris shortly. 'If so I should 'ave said so.'

Quest turned to Davidson.

'At least we have a description of one of the men concerned,' he said, 'and he shouldn't be difficult to find. He's not by any means an ordinary individual.'

'I'll have an 'All stations' call sent out directly I get back,' nodded the Inspector. 'I think I'll just have another look round in case there's anything I've overlooked, and then get along to the station.'

Philip Quest accompanied him on his tour of inspection, leaving the two girls together, but although they subjected the entire house to a close and thorough search, there was nothing to afford a clue to the identity of the intruder who had wrought such havoc.

The fog had cleared to a thin white vapour, half mist and half drizzle, when, after calling a constable and leaving him in charge, they took their departure.

Davidson suggested that Quest should come back with him to the police station, but the detective was tired, cold and hungry, and declined.

'I'll get back to my place,' he said. 'I want to think this affair thoroughly over. But I'll be back just before lunch time. If in the meantime you discover anything or there are any fresh developments, you might give me a ring.'

Inspector Davidson, obviously disappointed, promised, and the detective took his leave.

By the time he reached that part of the City, where his flat and office were situated, and had garaged the car, it was light, and the clatter of milk trollies heralded the coming day. He let himself into the flat and made his way through to the consulting-room. The maids were not yet up, and his partner, Richard Lester, was probably sleeping peacefully, unaware of the excitement which Quest had encountered during the day.

It had been pure chance that Quest had been at Sydenham at all the previous evening. A small matter had necessitated his seeing a friend of his who lived at Penge, and when he had started the fog had been nothing compared to that which he had run into later. The man he wanted to see had unfortunately been out, and the detective, rather disgusted at the futility of his journey and not relishing an immediate return through the thick blanket of yellow vapour that had suddenly descended, had bethought himself of his friend, Inspector Davidson, who was in charge of the Sydenham police station. Davidson had once been at the Yard, and it was during this period that Quest and he had become acquainted. The stout Inspector had been delighted, if more than surprised, to see his friend on such a night, and had welcomed him into his cosy office, and it was while they had been chatting and smoking before the banked up fire that Dr. Harman's call had come through.

The vague details that Davidson had gathered and passed on had sufficiently interested Quest for him to accompany the Inspector, and so, purely by accident, he had been pitchforked, as it were, into the beginnings of a mystery that was to tax all his ingenuity, and lead him into considerable danger before it was eventually solved.

The consulting-room looked cold and unprepossessing in the cold light of the early morning that filtered in between the half-drawn curtains. The ashes of a dead fire still littered the grate, and the papers that Lester had been reading thrown on the settee as he had left them when he went to bed.

Philip Quest, however, saw none of these things. His mind was fully occupied with the events of the evening, and before going to bed he wanted to straighten them out into something like order.

Tossing his hat and gloves on to a side

table, he lighted a cigarette and, still clad in his overcoat, dropped into a chair.

With eyes half closed and the grey-blue smoke curling upwards from the cigarette, he reviewed the vague facts which he had learned. Lamont, the elder, had been an engineer — something to do with mines in Johannesburg. He had returned apparently a rather morose man, with something weighing on his mind. At any rate, when he had come back he had not been the same as when he had gone away. According to his daughter he was taciturn and nervy — witness his agitation at the bursting of the motor-car tyre — and despite all questions, he refused to give any reason for this change of front. Six months after his return he gives to his daughter two finely worked veils, which he orders her to keep always in her possession, again without offering any reason for this, to say the least of it, peculiar behaviour. Prior to this incident he goes suddenly white at something in the paper, but there is no proof of this — and a week later is found hanging from a hook in his bedroom.

'And that,' murmured Quest to himself as he reached this point in his cogitations, 'is the end of part one.'

'Part two — if there is any connection — began last night. Let us see how this works out, and then try and fit part one and part two together.'

A man, unknown, calls on the son, and, by some means which is not yet known, entices him to the house where his father met his death and which is now unoccupied, and for some reason — also unknown — kills him. A short while after this another man — according to the maid it was another man — calls at the Lamonts' house, attacks and drugs the only person in charge, and makes a thorough search of the entire building without, apparently, taking anything. Now, the question was, how did this link up with the tragedy of the elder Lamont a year previously? Did it link up or was the killing of his son in the empty house merely a coincidence.

Quest unconsciously shook his head.

No, it was too much of a coincidence. There was a connection, and the thing to do was to find it. In spite of the girl's assertion that nothing had happened in Johannesburg to offer an explanation for the change in her father there must have been something, and it was this something that had laid the foundation stone for what had happened after. What was it that the elder Lamont had feared? Something that had suddenly become so imminent that the only escape was suicide.

Quest's hand strayed to his pocket and touched the envelope containing the two veils which he had brought away with him from the house in Park Road. How did these flimsy pieces of silk come into the business? There was — there must be — some hidden meaning attached to them despite their apparently innocent appearance, otherwise the girl's father would not have been so insistent that she kept them always with her. It was not unreasonable to suppose that the handing of them over to her had been prompted by something her father had read in the paper that morning, since it had occurred immediately after that incident. The first thing to do, he decided, was to look through the back files of that paper and study the copy that Lamont had been reading. Although the girl had found nothing there must be something, and perhaps his trained eye could find it.

There was one thing to be explained — the last words of the dying man in the empty house as recorded by Dr. Harman:

'Caught me — never guessed — the seventh — '

Who had caught him, and what had he never guessed? Never guessed that he was in danger, or never guessed the secret which probably he had learnt in that moment of dying? It was difficult to say. And the last words: 'The seventh.' The seventh — what?

The sound of clanking pails from below came to the detective's ears and warned him that his staff was up and beginning cleaning operations for the day. He rose and stretched himself stiffly. He had no intention of going to bed, but a bath and breakfast would remove that tiredness which his lack of sleep had brought about. He had at least checked over all the salient points of the problem, and probably before the day was out Davidson would have some news of the sallowfaced man who had called and taken Richard Lamont to his death.

Quest made his way to the bathroom, little dreaming that as he turned on the tap and undressed the man of whom he had been thinking had been found, and that Inspector Davidson was preparing to get on the telephone and acquaint him of the fact.

8

Crooks in Confidence

There is on the outskirts of Sydenham a maze of narrow, dirty, and mean-looking streets, lined on either side by narrow, dirty and mean-looking houses. Starting in Sydenham they spread and straggled into Penge like the tentacles of a gigantic octopus. The houses are inhabited by poor but respectable working class families, who eked out a depleted income by letting off one or more rooms. Such a family was the Wilkins family who occupied the 'estate premises and messuage' of No. 14, Tate Street.

Tate Street was slightly more pretentious than its neighbours, which is to say that its pavements were a little less cracked, its roadways in a trifle better state of repair, and its houses not quite in that state of dilapidation which characterised the others. Tate Street also boasted more than one lamp-post, a fact which brought joy to the hearts of its juvenile inhabitants, since it is very difficult to play a game of cricket properly with less than two of these necessary adjuncts.

That the lights in these lamp-posts were generally out owing to the enthusiasm of these same youthful inhabitants did nothing to detract from their usefulness, and indeed was a great consolation to some of the people who lived in that salubrious thoroughfare. For although Tate Street was for the greater part, respectable, it is to be feared that some of the denizens who slunk back to lay their weary bodies down upon the narrow beds in the small and stuffy rooms that constituted their homes were anything but respectable. The majority had occupations that allowed them to sleep for most of the day and only venture forth under cover of darkness, and these occupations are better not enquired into too closely.

On that evening when the fog lay thickly like a white woollen blanket over everything, and Richard Lamont left his home in Park Road with his unknown escort, never to return, the lodger who occupied the top front room in the Wilkins establishment came home late.

He came furtively in spite of the fact that the street was deserted owing to the blinding fog, and, letting himself in with his key, noiselessly mounted the rickety stairs to his room. It was not a large room, neither was it luxuriously appointed, but it was scrupulously clean and to a certain degree comfortable.

Its tenant closed the door carefully and lighted the gas. The hands of a cheap clock on the mantelpiece pointed to a quarter past twelve as he divested himself of his shabby coat, and crossing the room, pulled up the torn blind. For a moment he peered out into the opaque whiteness of the fog, though since he could see nothing it appeared rather a waste of time, and then, going to a cupboard, he unlocked it, and, producing a bottle and a glass, poured himself out a stiff tot of whisky and gulped it down.

The spirit warmed his frozen body and he repeated the action before setting down the empty glass.

A peculiar man, this top-floor front lodger. A man of medium height with a wizened face that vice had marked with deep lines and given an age that years did not warrant. For in spite of the deeply graven lines and wrinkles this man was not old. He was, in fact, barely over thirty, but he might easily have passed for sixty. His hair, when he removed his cap, was thin and grey — a grey in which was mingled streaks of jet black that gave to his appearance a strange pie-bald look. His nose was thin and reddish-coloured, in strong contrast to the pale, unhealthy hue of his face, and the eyes, small and bead-like, were set so close to the bridge that they were almost lost in its shadow.

If ever nature shrieked a warning concerning the character of a human being in its outward appearance, she did so in this case. And yet there was one redeeming feature — a feature that was as incongruous as it was unexpected. His hands were singularly beautiful — the hands of an artist or a musician. Long, slim, white, and beautifully kept, they looked as if they should have belonged to somebody else — that their present owner had no right to them.

For some time he walked up and down the room impatiently, stopping every now and then at the window and listening intently. But it was nearly one o'clock before the sound he was evidently expecting broke the stillness of the fog-shrouded night — a low, soft whistle.

With an exclamation of mingled satisfaction and impatience the tenant of the bed-sitting room went swiftly to the door and passed out on to the dark landing. With infinite care he made his way down the stairs and gently opened the front door. A dark figure loomed on the step, and wisps of fog curled into the narrow passage.

'Come on,' whispered the man who had opened the door, 'and don't make a noise. I don't want the household to know you've been.'

The visitor grunted and stepped across the threshold, waiting while the other re-closed the door. There was a little click, and a white shaft of light sprung from the bulbous end of a torch and waved on the foot of the staircase.

'Go up,' hissed the man who held it, 'and be careful of the fifth stair, it creaks like Hades!'

The man who had called at this late hour moved forward, and his tall figure, getting in the way of the rays of the torch, sent an elongated, distorted shadow, slanting up the dingy wall.

In single file they mounted the stairs and entered the top front room. The man with the beautiful hands snapped off the torch and slipped it back in his pocket. As he closed the door the newcomer spoke for the first time.

'Well,' he said quickly, 'did you get it?'

The other shook his head.

'Why?' The question came abruptly, angrily, like the report from a pistol.

'Because it wasn't there,' answered the tenant of the room.

'Wasn't there?' The visitor took a step forward. 'Nonsense! It must be there. You overlooked it.'

'I tell you it wasn't there,' said the other sullenly. 'I searched the place thoroughly.

If it had been there I should have found it.'

The visitor muttered an oath.

'You can't have looked everywhere, Merrick,' he snarled. 'I tell you I'm sure those veils were in the house. They couldn't have been anywhere else.'

'Well, they weren't there,' replied Merrick. 'You don't suppose I'm such a fool that I'd go to all the trouble and risk I did go to, and then come away without getting what I went for if the things had been there! If you do you'd better have another suppose. Unless there's some secret hiding place in the house I give you my word that those veils are not there.'

The visitor frowned and thoughtfully rubbed his finger and thumb together.

'What the devil can he have done with them?' he muttered savagely. 'I made sure they were there — '

'Perhaps the old man destroyed them,' began Merrick, pouring out another drink.

'The old man gave them to his daughter, we know that,' snapped the other. 'Have you got another glass? I'll have some of that.'

Without replying Merrick went over to the cupboard and produced a second glass, which he brought over to the table. The visitor picked up the bottle and poured himself out a large whisky.

'We know that he gave those veils to the girl,' he said, after he had sipped at his drink, 'and if they're not in the house she must have done something with them.' He drained his glass and set it down. 'We've got to get them. They are essential to the scheme.'

'If the girl knows where they are,' said Merrick, tapping gently on the table with his long, white fingers and looking meaningly at the other, 'it shouldn't be difficult to make her tell us.'

The visitor regarded him steadily.

'That, I think, is the best way,' he replied. 'We should have done that in the beginning.' He looked round, drew forward a chair and sat down. 'Let's talk it over,' he said.

It was nearly two hours later when Merrick softly let his visitor out and watched his tall figure disappear into the thinning fog. Not so very far away at that precise moment Celia Lamont was telling Philip Quest all she knew of the two veils which her father had entrusted to her care, oblivious of the fact that there had been hatched against her a plot that was to menace reason and almost life itself!

9

A Second Murder!

After a bathe, a shave and a change of clothing, Philip Quest found that his tiredness had almost completely disappeared and had been replaced by hunger.

As he came out of his bedroom he saw the figure of Lester just entering the bathroom, and called a cheery good morning. Richard paused.

'Hullo!' he said. 'What time did you get in last night? It must have been pretty late. I waited up until nearly one.'

'It was very early, to be exact,' answered the detective. 'Almost daylight.'

'What happened?' asked Lester. 'Did you get held up with the fog.'

'Something more interesting than that,' replied Quest. 'I'll tell you all about it at breakfast.'

Lester disappeared into the bathroom and the detective went into the dining room. From somewhere came the smell of coffee and the fragrance of grilling bacon. His hand was on the handle of the door when the telephone bell in the consulting-room shrilled loudly. Quest crossed the passage, went in, and picked up the receiver.

'Hullo!' called an excited voice. 'Is that Mr. Quest?'

'Speaking,' answered the detective. 'What is it, Davidson?'

'We've found that fellow — the Spanish-looking man that the maid described,' bellowed the Inspector.

'Oh, you have, have you?' said Quest interestedly. 'That's mighty quick work, Davidson. What's he got to say for himself?'

'He hasn't got anything to say for himself,' came the reply. 'He's dead!'

'Dead!' snapped Quest, and his eyes narrowed. 'How did he die?'

'He was stabbed in the back,' said Davidson, and went on to describe how and where the man had been found.

It appeared that a patrolling policeman, on his beat in Elm Tree Avenue in the early hours of the morning, had suddenly come upon a great splash of blood on the pavement. It was obviously fresh and still wet, and at first the man had been puzzled as to how it had got there. Looking about him, however, he had seen that a trail of spots led towards the closed gate of a house a few yards away. It was an empty house, and under a clump of bushes in the front garden the policeman had found the dead body of the man. There was no doubt that it was a case of murder, for the knife with which he had been done to death still stuck out between his shoulder blades.

The constable had informed his sergeant, who had communicated with the police station, and from the description of the murdered man Davidson had at once recognised the man whom Doris had described as having called for Richard Lamont.

He had gone at once to the scene of the crime, calling on his way for the maid and taking her with him. She had at once identified the body as being that of the Spanish-looking man who had called for her master on the previous night.

An inspection of the pockets revealed the fact that they had been rifled, but in the inside breast pocket part of an envelope had been discovered bearing the name 'Manuel Souza.' There was no address, for the envelope had apparently never been through the post, but had been delivered by hand.

'I wish you could come along, Mr. Quest,' concluded the Inspector. 'The body hasn't been moved and everything is exactly as we found it. If you could possibly come right away I should like your opinion.'

'I'll come immediately I've had breakfast,' said Quest. 'Meet me at the police station.'

He hung up the receiver and turned as Lester, glowing from his bath and fully dressed, entered.

'The breakfast has just gone in,' he exclaimed, 'and I can do with it. I'm starving.'

'There's nothing very new in that,' said Quest. 'But you'll have to be quick and get through it as soon as possible. We've got to be away in ten minutes.'

Lester stared at him.

'Away?' he echoed. 'Where are we going to?'

'Sydenham,' replied the detective, leading the way towards the dining room. 'Don't waste time now asking questions. I'll tell you all about it on the way.'

They had a hurried meal, and then went round to the garage and got out the car. The fog of the night before had given place to a thin, unpleasant drizzle, and the streets looked grey and uninviting. Under Quest's skilful hand the big car was sent speeding through the West End, and once they were clear of the dense traffic the detective began to give his friend and partner an account of his last night's adventures.

'Gosh!' he exclaimed, when he had heard the whole story. 'You've run up against a problem this time!'

The detective nodded.

'Yes,' he remarked. 'It's rather a pretty little mystery, and I must confess that I'm more than usually interested.'

Before Lester could say any more he

had sent the car gliding into the kerb and brought it to a halt outside the police station.

Davidson had evidently been on the lookout for them, for Quest had barely descended from the driving seat before the stout Inspector appeared at the top of the short flight of steps.

'You haven't been long,' he greeted, and grinned cheerfully at Lester. 'Hullo! It's a long time since I saw you.'

Lester looked at him critically.

'You don't look so well as you used to,' he said. 'What have you been doing, dieting?'

Davidson's red face deepened to crimson.

'You haven't changed, have you?' he grunted. 'You cheeky youngster.'

'When you've finished being rude to each other,' interposed Quest with a smile, 'perhaps we can get to business. I should like to go along to where this man was found at once.'

Inspector Davidson was in full agreement with this suggestion, and, after leaving word with the desk sergeant where he could be found, got into Quest's car with the detective and Lester.

It didn't take them long to reach Elm Tree Avenue, and as they turned into the road it was easy to distinguish the house they were seeking. It was about two hundred yards further down on the same side as that of the empty house in which Richard Lamont had been killed. A 'To Let' board protruded drunkenly from the uncut straggling hedge that bordered the front garden, and by the gate stood the impassive figure of a uniformed policeman, gazing with displeasure at a small group of sightseers who lounged on the pavement.

The constable saluted as Quest brought the car to a standstill in front of the gate, and the loungers gaped and became imbued with renewed interest at the prospect of a further free show.

Davidson was the first to alight, and he led the way across the strip of wet pavement and opened the gate.

'The body is over there, Mr. Quest,' he said in a low voice, pointing to a semi-circular patch of low shrubbery that grew beside the path leading up to the house. Philip Quest followed the direction of his finger, and saw the soles of two shoes, pathetically still, protruding from the mass evergreens.

Without comment he went over and gazed down at the sprawling figure. It lay face upwards on the wet ground, half hidden by a screen of leaves. The eyes were closed and the face almost calm and peaceful. Death had evidently come quite unexpectedly.

'This is exactly how you found him?' asked the detective, without turning.

Davidson shook his head.

'Not exactly,' he replied. 'He was moved slightly by the Divisional Surgeon when he made his examination.'

'I see.' Quest stooped. 'Hold these branches back, will you, Lester?'

Lester complied, and kneeling by the body the detective turned it gently over. A dark-coloured patch became visible on the back of the coat, in the centre of which was a narrow clean cut.

'We removed the knife,' said the Inspector. 'I've got it at the station if you want to see it. I'm having it tested for fingerprints.'

Quest nodded abstractedly.

'Of course,' he said. 'The murder was not committed here in the garden. He was killed outside in the street and his body dragged in here after. You can see the marks that his heels have made in the gravel.'

'That was my opinion, too,' said Davidson. 'That would account for the blood on the pavement.'

'Yes.' The detective raised each leg gently and examined the back of the heels of the shoes. 'If any further confirmation was necessary it is here in the scratched and torn leather. You say you searched the pockets thoroughly?'

'Yes,' nodded the Inspector. 'There was nothing in them except a bunch of keys, his watch, and the scrap of envelope with his name.'

'And they had obviously been rifled.'

'Most of them had been turned inside out,' said Davidson. 'There's no doubt that the murderer made a thorough search.'

'Regarding that envelope, I think you are rather jumping to conclusions,' remarked Quest. 'You conclude that because it was found in his pocket and bears a name that name is necessarily his own?'

'Well, I don't know,' said Davidson. 'He's obviously a foreigner, and the name is a Spanish name — '

'Oh, I agree that it's a probability,' broke in the detective, 'but it's by no means a certainty. However, it shouldn't be difficult to make sure one way or the other.'

He stopped abruptly. While he had been speaking his long, sensitive fingers had been dipping in and out of the dead man's pockets. Now he paused, and across his face flashed an expression of sudden alertness. Lester, who was watching closely, stepped forward.

'What is it?' he asked. 'You've found something?'

Philip Quest made no reply, but picking up one of the cold and stiff hands that lay outflung from the body, he peered at the clenched fingers.

'I believe I have,' he muttered softly, and began to prise loose those gripped fingers. It took him some time, but at last he had the dead hand open. There fell from the palm a square of white — a crumpled card.

'What is it, sir?' cried Davidson.

'It's a visiting card,' replied the detective gravely, and stared at the printed name and address:

James Harding,
   17, Uppingham Road, Sydenham,
      S.E.I.

The name and address of the man whom Celia Lamont had mentioned on the previous night!

10

Gone!

The fat face of Inspector Davidson was clouded as he gazed over Philip Quest's shoulder at the crumpled card.

'I don't know how I came to miss that,' he muttered, shaking his head. 'It was careless of me — very careless.'

'It wasn't very conspicuous,' said Quest. 'I only saw it by accident. I just caught a gleam of white from between his fingers.' He handed the card to the Inspector. 'You'd better take charge of that,' he went on. 'I think as soon as we've finished here our next move will be to call on Mr. James Harding and find out what he knows about this affair.'

Davidson agreed and pocketed the card, standing frowning thoughtfully while Philip Quest continued his investigations. The detective, however, found nothing more, and presently he straightened up.

'You can send for the ambulance now and have him taken to the mortuary,' he said, 'and it would be a good idea to try and find out where he lived. I should like to know all about him and who his friends were.'

He walked thoughtfully to the car while the Inspector issued his instructions to the constable, and when Davidson joined him he looked up.

'Whereabouts is Uppingham Road?' he asked a little abruptly.

Davidson explained, and Quest sent the big car gliding away, to the intense disappointment of the group of sensation seekers who still hung about the gateway of the empty house.

Uppingham Road was a broad thoroughfare turning off the High Street, and number seventeen proved to be a large house that had been converted into flats. Judging by the row of four highly polished bell pushes, there were four flats in all, and over a third of these was a neat plate bearing the name James Harding.

Philip Quest pressed the bell under this plate and waited. There was a long pause, and then the front door was opened by a girl — evidently a servant.

'I wish to see Mr. James Harding,' said Quest pleasantly, as the servant gazed at him enquiringly.

'Third floor,' was the laconic reply, and followed by Lester and Davidson, the detective stepped into the hall. The door was closed behind them, and with a muttered 'Step this way,' the girl began to ascend the stairs.

The three of them followed her to a green painted door on the third landing at which she knocked.

It was opened almost at once by a figure in a blue silk dressing gown, who protruded his head and enquired:

'What is it, Emma?'

'Gentlemen,' replied Emma, briefly, and made her way down the stairs again. Mr. Harding regarded his visitors questioningly.

'You wished to see me?' he asked in a deep, rather mellow voice.

Philip Quest constituted himself the spokesman of the party.

'We should like to have a few words

with you, Mr. Harding,' he said. 'My name is Philip Quest — this is Inspector Davidson — '

'Oh,' broke in the man in the dressing gown, and a flash of understanding crossed his face. 'I see. It's about Dick Lamont, I suppose? Come in.'

He stood aside and ushered them into the tiny hall of the flat.

'I heard all about it from Celia — er — Miss Lamont, this morning. She rang me up.' He pushed open a door on the right and led the way into a pleasant room that was half sitting room and half study. 'Shocking affair, isn't it? Won't you sit down?'

He waved his head towards a group of easy chairs by the fireside.

'It's a very nasty business,' replied Quest. 'You have, I understand, known the Lamonts for a long time?'

Harding nodded. He was a tall, bronzed man, with crisp, curling fair hair and blue eyes. Quest put his age at a little over thirty, and discovered later that he was in fact thirty-three. He gave the impression of perfect physical fitness — a man who in a tight corner would be able to give a good account of himself.

'Yes, I've known the family for nearly five years,' he said, extracting a cigarette from a case that he took out of his dressing-gown pocket and carefully lighting it.

'Then you may be able to tell us something that will throw a light on the mystery,' said Quest. 'What we're trying to discover at the moment is some sort of motive — '

'I'm afraid if you are relying on me to supply you with that you're going to be disappointed,' Harding broke in. 'I can suggest no reason why anyone should want to kill young Lamont.'

Quest watched him steadily, and the blue eyes returned his gaze without flinching.

'The death of the father was an unfortunate affair, too,' he said after a slight pause. 'I was wondering if there could be any connection.'

A momentary change took place in the bronzed face before him — a little flicker of — surprise? Alarm? Fear? — Quest

116

could not be quite certain. Perhaps a combination of all three. It was gone in an instant, and when Harding spoke there was no trace in his voice of that momentary agitation.

'I don't see how there could be any connection,' he said easily. 'Mr. Lamont committed suicide. It was very dreadful, but there was no mystery about it.'

He leaned towards a small table, and neatly deposited the ash from his cigarette in a bronze bowl.

'Why did he commit suicide?' asked Quest quietly.

Harding shrugged his broad shoulders.

'I don't know,' he replied shortly.

'Then,' continued the detective, 'you can hardly say that there was no mystery about it, can you?'

The other shot him a quick, suspicious glance.

'Well, no — if you put it like that,' he said. 'What I meant was that it — his death — was not due to anyone else — like Dick's. In other words, he wasn't murdered.'

He was losing his calmness. Quest

117

noticed that the hand that raised the half-smoked cigarette to his lips was trembling.

'There are other ways of killing a man than by a knife or a bullet,' he said meaningly. 'It is possible to — frighten a man to death.'

Again came that momentary flicker of fear in the other's eyes. This man Harding knew something. He inhaled deeply at his cigarette, and when he spoke again the words were obviously to gain time.

'Frighten a man to death?' he repeated slowly. 'I don't understand what you mean?'

Philip Quest gave a slight twitch to his shoulders.

'I will try and put it plainer,' he said. 'From what I heard from Miss Lamont her father was in a state of considerable nervous agitation for some time before he died. If — and I am only suggesting this — somebody was scaring him — frightening him to such an extent that death seemed the only way out, the sequel which followed was practically a foregone conclusion.'

Mr. Harding examined the ash on the glowing end of his cigarette intently.

'It seems rather a far-fetched conclusion,' he said at length. 'Who would be in a position to frighten Lamont to such an extent, and how were they able to do it?'

'That is what I want to find out,' said the detective. 'I was hoping you would be able to help me.'

The other raised his eyebrows.

'Why should you think I can help you,' he demanded.

'Because you know of something that happened in Johannesburg to Lamont that you haven't told,' snapped Quest quickly.

It was a shot in the dark, prompted by the general behaviour of the man before him, but it hit the mark. Harding's face whitened and the stub of the cigarette fell from his fingers and hit the hearthrug with a little shower of sparks. He stooped quickly and picked it up, crushing it out in the bronze ash bowl. When he turned to face Quest again he had, to a certain extent, recovered his composure.

'I'm afraid you are labouring under a

delusion,' he said coolly. 'Where or how you got your information I don't know and I don't care, but it's all wrong, entirely wrong. I know of nothing that happened to Lamont in Johannesburg that bears out your rather vivid imagination.'

Quest smiled. He was certain that Harding was lying, but he had expected little else. He had lied to Celia Lamont, and therefore it was unlikely that he would tell the truth to a stranger, even though that stranger was a man with his — Quest's — reputation. The question was — why had he lied?

'You made enquiries, I believe, for Miss Lamont at the time?' he said, and Harding nodded.

'I did,' he replied. 'I suppose she told you?'

'Yes,' said Quest.

'And I suppose also,' continued Harding, 'that she told you my enquiries yielded no results?'

'She did,' answered the detective.

'Then I fail to see' — Harding helped himself to another cigarette — 'I fail to see why you should have come to the erroneous conclusion that I did discover something?'

'Was it erroneous?' said Quest mildly.

Harding's lips set dangerously and his eyes flashed.

'I am not accustomed to having my word doubted,' he snapped. 'I have told you that I know nothing, and if you don't choose to believe me we may as well put an end to this interview at once. Good morning!'

He stalked to the door and held it open.

'Just a minute,' said the detective easily. 'Mr. Harding, this is not a question of whether one person believes another person's word or not. This is a much more serious business than that. We are here to enquire into a case of murder, not to play a game of believe or disbelieve. It may give you a great deal of moral satisfaction to behave in this melodramatic manner, but it doesn't help us to find the murderer of Richard Lamont.'

A dull red flush suffused the pale cheeks of the man by the door. For a second he stared at the detective, and then, slamming the door, he came back to his previous position before the fireplace.

'I apologise,' he said curtly. 'But you rather got my back up. Go ahead with what you want, and if I can help you I will.'

Quest noticed the slight stress he had laid on the 'can.' It could be interpreted in two ways.

'Do you know a man named Manuel Souza?' he asked abruptly.

Harding was unprepared for the question. He had expected the conversation to be continued on the same lines as it had left off, and this unexpected twist took him completely by surprise. His expression was a mixture of astonishment, doubt, and incredulity.

'Yes, I do,' he answered. 'But how the dickens you know I do, beats me.'

'Do you know him well?' said Quest, ignoring the latter part of the other's remark.

Harding shook his head.

'No. As a matter of fact, I've only met him twice in my life,' he replied. 'Why?'

'He was found dead at an early hour this morning in the garden of an empty house in Elm Tree Avenue,' answered the detective, watching the other closely.

'Good heavens!' Harding made no effort to conceal his horror and surprise. 'Dead! How did he die?'

Unless he was a particularly good actor his horror and surprise were genuine. Quest decided that whatever else he might know, this was the first intimation he had received of Manuel Souza's death.

'He was murdered,' said Quest quietly. 'Like Richard Lamont!'

'Stabbed?' The question came with a little hissing rush of breath from between clenched teeth and bloodless lips.

Quest nodded.

Harding's face was ashen, and every effort he made to restore his calmness was futile. The news had shocked him — shaken him to his soul.

'He didn't expect that,' was the detective's mental comment as he watched. 'I wonder if it will make him speak?'

He was not to wonder long. Harding passed his tongue over his lips and cleared his throat as though to relax the taut muscles.

'This is terrible — dreadful,' he said huskily. 'Why — it was only yesterday afternoon — ' He broke off.

'What was only yesterday afternoon?' prompted the detective.

'It was only yesterday afternoon that he — he came here to see me,' said Harding almost inaudibly.

There was a moment's silence. Lester looked at Davidson and Davidson looked at Quest. The stout Inspector opened his mouth and shut it again with a snap. It was Philip Quest who spoke.

'Who was Manuel Souza?' he asked, 'and why did he come here to see you?'

The expression of Harding's face changed. The colour came slowly back and the horror faded from the eyes. When he replied his voice had regained its firmness.

'Manuel Souza was Mr. Lamont's assistant in Johannesburg,' he said. 'Why he came to see me I refuse to discuss.'

Philip Quest's face set sternly.

'I suppose you realise,' he said, 'that by

withholding information that may lead to the arrest of the person or persons responsible for these murders you are laying yourself open to a charge — the charge of accessory to the crimes either before or after the fact!'

Harding's jaw thrust forward at a stubborn angle.

'Is that a definite charge?' he demanded.

'Not at the moment,' retorted Quest. 'But if you still persist in your attitude it can be made one.'

Harding's blue eyes met the gaze of Quest's steely grey ones without flinching.

'I'm afraid in any case it makes no difference,' he said. 'The reason Souza came to see me is a private one and I cannot divulge it.'

The detective shrugged his shoulders.

'You are aware, of course,' he said, 'that according to Miss Lamont's maid it was Souza who called for Richard Lamont on the night he met his death?'

Harding nodded.

'Yes, I am aware of that,' he replied. 'In fact, he borrowed my car for the purpose.'

'Your car?' Quest's eyes narrowed. 'Is the number XV 6094?'

Again Harding nodded.

'That's the number of the car that was found abandoned in the front garden of the house in Elm Tree Avenue,' put in Inspector Davidson, speaking for the first time.

'Yes, that was mine,' said Harding shortly.

Philip Quest's hand went to the breast-pocket of his coat and took out his wallet. From it he extracted a sheet of torn paper.

'Have you ever seen this before?' he asked.

Harding came forward and glanced at it. It was the paper they had found in the dashboard compartment of the deserted car.

'Of course I have,' he replied casually. 'I wrote it.'

Inspector Davidson stiffened, caught Quest's eye and relaxed again. The detective carefully replaced the slip of paper in his wallet and put it back in his pocket.

'Mr. Harding,' he said. 'Don't you think that all this requires explanation? You gave this man, Souza, Richard Lamont's address. You informed him that Lamont had the key — presumably the key of the empty house. Souza took him to that house in your car, and in that house he was stabbed to death — '

'Souza had nothing to do with that,' interposed Harding quickly.

'How do you know that?' snapped Quest. 'He called for Lamont and he took him to the house. How do you know he did not commit the murder?'

'Because he had no reason for doing so,' said Harding. 'He took him to the house because — ' He stopped abruptly.

'Because what?' said the detective.

'I can't tell you that,' said Harding, and the stubborn look appeared on his face once more.

'Can't or won't?' rapped Quest.

'Which ever you like,' retorted the other.

The detective felt his temper rising, but he crushed it down and outwardly remained calm. Harding was a stubborn young fool, but he was a fool who would not be browbeaten. Quest recognised the type. You might be able to lead him but you'd never drive him.

'I think you're being very foolish, Mr. Harding,' he said smoothly. 'If you know anything about this business — and it is fairly evident that you do — it is your duty as a law-abiding citizen to help the police.'

'I can't add anything to what I have already said,' replied Harding. 'If it were possible I would help you, but under the circumstances it is not.'

'What are the circumstances?' persisted Quest, but the other shook his head.

'I can't tell you that, either,' he said doggedly.

'You fully realise the consequences that will follow this attitude of yours?' said Quest. 'This is a serious business involving two murders, and you are withholding evidence likely to lead to the arrest of the guilty parties. That, in the eyes of the law, is a very grave offence, in fact, it is criminal.'

'I can't help it,' said Harding. 'I've

nothing more to say. You must do as you think fit.'

'That is your last word?' said Quest.

'That is my last word,' was the reply.

Quest turned to Inspector Davidson and shrugged his shoulders.

'I'm afraid I shall have to ask you to accompany me to the station, sir,' said the fat Inspector officially. 'I'm sorry, but you've brought it on yourself.'

'Does that mean that I'm under arrest?' said Harding. He spoke steadily but his face was pale, and his hands trembled slightly.

'No,' answered Davidson. 'It means that you will be detained on suspicion pending further enquiries.'

'That's practically the same thing,' snapped Harding impatiently. 'Will you allow me to go to my dressing room and change. I can hardly come with you like this.'

The Inspector agreed courteously, and Harding left the room.

'Well, what do you make of it, Mr. Quest?' asked Davidson in a low voice, moving over to the door so that he could keep an eye on the corridor.

'I don't know, Davidson,' replied Quest frowning. 'And that's being perfectly candid. Harding knows a lot, but why he won't tell what he knows rather puzzles me.'

'Unless he's the guilty person — ' began Lester, but Quest shook his head.

'He's not guilty of the murders, unless he's mad,' he said. 'Nobody but a madman would behave as he is doing if he were guilty. No, I don't think he's the murderer, but I'm convinced that he knows who is and the motive behind the whole business.'

'Then he's screening someone,' said Lester. 'That must be the explanation.'

'That's what I think,' agreed Quest. 'The question is — who?'

'What about the girl?' suggested Davidson. 'She appears to be friendly with him, more than friendly by appearances.'

Quest nodded. He remembered the flush that had dyed Celia Lamont's cheeks when she had mentioned Harding's name. But if Harding was shielding her she must in some way be guilty of her brother's death, and that was almost incredible. And yet — Further train of thought was interrupted by the appearance of Harding minus the blue dressing gown and clad now in a neat grey suit. He carried a raincoat and hat.

'I'm ready if you are,' he said briefly, and a few seconds later they were in Quest's car *en route* for the police station.

'I won't come in just now,' said the detective in answer to Davidson's invitation. 'There's a call I want to make. I'll see you later.'

He waited until the short form of the Inspector and his virtual prisoner had disappeared within the entrance, and then sent the big car gliding forward again.

'Where are we going?' asked Lester as they swung round into the side street.

'We are going to Park Road,' replied Philip Quest. 'I'm rather anxious to see Celia Lamont's reaction when I tell her that Harding has been detained under suspicion.'

But his anxiety was destined not to be fulfilled, for in answer to his enquiry a puzzled Doris informed him that her mistress was out.

'You know she is,' said the servant.

'I know!' Quest raised his eyebrows. 'I know now you've told me — '

'But yer must 'ave known before yer came 'ere,' said the girl. 'Seein' as 'ow yer sent the keb fer 'er.'

'Cab — what cab?' snapped Quest, and a sudden feeling of alarm took possession of him.

'The taxi — it came about an hour ago,' said Doris. 'Man brought a note asking Miss Celia to meet you at the 'ouse in Elm Tree Avenue.'

'Did she go?' broke in the detective.

''Course she went!' said Doris, and then, as she saw Quest's expression: ''Ere, didn't yer send that keb?'

But Philip Quest was no longer listening. With an abrupt movement he had turned away and was hurrying back to where he had left his car.

11

What Happened to Celia

Like Philip Quest, Celia Lamont got very little sleep that night following the discovery of her brother's death in the empty house. When Davidson and the detective had gone she drank some tea brought to her by a solicitous Doris, and went up to bed. Her senses were still in the numbed, dazed state that she had explained to Quest, but through the deadening effect of the shock were coming little twinges of realisation, like the awakening of a nerve that has been deadened by cocaine. And these recurrent twinges kept her wakeful and restless throughout the rest of the night, so that she welcomed the first grey of dawn with a sigh of thankfulness.

By seven o'clock she was up and dressed and wandering disconsolately about the dismantled house trying to accustom herself to these new conditions which Fate, in the guise of violent death, had subjected her to. She had the unpleasant feeling of having lived through all this before, of knowing exactly what she was going to do and feel and say next, and remembered that she had felt just like this after the suicide of her father.

At half-past eight she rang up James Harding and poured out her troubles into his sympathetic ear. He promised to come round during the morning, and, feeling a little better for the sound of his voice and the knowledge that there was still someone in the world to whom she could turn, Celia made a half-hearted attempt to eat the breakfast that Doris had prepared for her.

She managed to nibble at some toast and drink two cups of coffee, and then, in the hope that the occupation would prevent her thinking, set about helping to put the disordered house straight. And she was so engaged when the taxi arrived.

The driver, whom Mrs. Wilkins would have recognised as her top floor lodger, presented a note which she opened. The envelope contained a sheet of paper torn from a pocket-book on which were scrawled several lines of pencilled writing.

'Will you come at once in the cab to Elm Tree Avenue. I have found something which I should like you to explain.

'PHILIP QUEST.'

With no suspicion that the message was anything but what it seemed, Celia hastily put on her hat and coat, told Doris where she was going, and followed the driver to the waiting car. He held open the door for her and she got in. She heard the door close with a thud followed by the tinkling crash of breaking glass, and then she seemed to slide away on a sea of darkness into oblivion!

★　★　★

When the first glimmer of returning consciousness began to percolate through that veil of velvet blackness, Celia's brain registered the thought that she had fainted.

This conviction became more and more certain as she regained the full use of her senses. She remembered getting into the cab, the slamming door, and then — nothing. The strain of the previous night and the excitement of Quest's note must have been too much for her. Stupid thing to do, she thought as she tried to concentrate her scattered wits. However, she could not have remained unconscious for long, because she was still in the cab. Just a momentary lapse, that was all it was.

She had slipped sideways into one corner, and now she made an effort and sat up. The movement sent the blood pounding through her veins and caused her head to ache so violently that she could scarcely see. When the pain subsided a little and her vision cleared she looked out of the window — and then what she saw set her heart leaping with alarm.

The cab was running at considerable speed between high hedges beyond which lay a wide expanse of ploughed fields. They were in the open country!

Celia shut her eyes. This must be a dream, she concluded. It couldn't be real. The distance from her own house to Elm Tree Avenue was quite a short one, and there was certainly nothing in the nature of country in between. She must still be unconscious and imagining those flying hedges and desolate brown fields.

She opened her eyes again. If this was a dream it was a very vivid one. There was nothing hazy or unreal about the vista that was visible through the window. This was no imagination.

But what did it all mean, and where was she being taken? Had that message really come from Philip Quest, or —

Feeling thoroughly alarmed, Celia Lamont leaned forward and tapped sharply on the glass of the window that divided the interior of the cab from the broad back of the driver. He looked round, grinned and stopped the cab. She saw him climb down from behind the wheel, and as he came round to the door she became aware for the first time of a peculiar sickly smell that filled the confined space of the cab. Like the switching on of a revealing light she heard again the soft crash of breaking glass that had accompanied the closing of the door. She looked down. On the fibre mat that covered the floor she saw a little scattered collection of glistening particles. And then the full realisation of what had happened burst upon her. She hadn't fainted — she had been drugged! The closing of the door had broken a thin glass tube containing some form of gas or volatile drug.

The driver of the cab jerked open the right-hand door and stood grinning at her.

'Recovered, have you?' he grunted. 'I thought it was about time you did.'

She looked at him, her eyes wide with fear.

'Why have you brought me here?' she asked huskily. 'Where are you taking me?'

'You'll see all in good time,' he retorted. 'In the meantime, now you've got back to your senses, I'm going to tie you up in case you should try any tricks.'

He hauled out of his pocket a length of thin cord, and, leaning forward, gripped her wrists. She made an attempt to struggle, but his strength was enormous, and with a few swift turns he secured her hands, and carrying the cord down did the same to her ankles. When he had knotted the ends she was helpless.

'I'll fix it so that you can't scream, and then I think you'll do for the time being,' he said, whipping out a handkerchief from his pocket and binding it tightly round her mouth. 'There, now you're all nice and comfy!'

Completely powerless, she watched him close the door and return to the front of the cab. He had left the engine running, and, climbing up into the driving seat, he pressed his foot on the clutch pedal, jerked at the gear lever, and they moved forward again on the way to this unknown destination.

At least, unknown as far as Celia was concerned. Where was she being taken, and what awaited her at the end of the journey? That she was in the hands of the man who had killed Dick there was little room for doubt. But what did he want with her? Why had they taken this trouble to kidnap her? What lay behind this outrage? She naturally connected it with the death of her father, and the fear which had consumed him just prior to his suicide, but what it was all about she hadn't the least idea. Was this man who was driving her so swiftly along the winding road the man of whom he had been afraid? Or were there others? She concluded that it was useless speculating concerning this. She would find out when they arrived wherever they were going.

She began to wonder if Philip Quest would learn of what had occurred, and decided that of course he would, and with this knowledge came a little ray of hope. She didn't quite know what he could do, but she felt that he would do something. She was terribly frightened — the more so because what lay ahead of her was unknown.

The journey seemed endless. For the most part they kept to the open country road, but every now and again they passed through a small town or village.

She had no idea of the locality or which county they were in, but the countryside seemed to grow more wild and desolate as they proceeded.

Presently the cab swung off the main road to the left and began to bump its way over the rutted surface of a narrow lane. At the end of this lane was a broken gate that stood open, and she saw beyond a dirty yard in which some chickens were running about pecking among the refuse. Several disreputable outhouses came into view, and then the low lines of a straggling building of white stone that looked like a farm house. Before the back door of this place the cab stopped and the driver sounded his horn three times. There was a pause, and then the door opened and a woman appeared. A thin-faced woman, dirty and ill-kempt, with stray wisps of greying hair that blew about her unprepossessing face. Her nose was reddish purple and her eyes were small and watery.

She greeted the driver of the cab in a high, querulous voice that was almost a whine.

'Oh, you've got 'ere, 'ave you?'

'Looks like it, doesn't it?' he replied, getting down. 'Has the boss arrived yet?'

The woman nodded, her ferrety eyes peering into the cab at the girl.

''E's with the doctor,' she said. 'Is this the girl? Are you going to take her in to them?'

'What d'yer think I'm going to do — leave her here?' snapped the other. ''Course I'm going to take her in!'

The woman muttered something as he pulled open the door and stooping forward, picked Celia up in his arms.

'Come along, my girl,' he said. 'This is going to be your future home. I hope you'll like it.'

He carried her over to the back door and entered a passage. At the top of four steps the passage widened, and he kicked open a door on the right. The room beyond was almost square, with a low ceiling, and furnished shabbily but comfortably. A coal fire burned in the grate and the air was stuffy and fetid as though the window were seldom opened.

A man clad in a dingy dressing gown

142

who had been seated by the fire, rose at their entrance. Celia thought she had never seen a more repulsive-looking person. He was almost completely bald, with a large drooping nose that jutted out over loose, wet and over-red lips. His hands were bony, the skin greasy and the nails black with dirt, and they shook as though their owner suffered with palsy.

'Here you are, Doctor, here she is,' said the cab driver, laying the girl down on the dingy sofa.

The old man came over, and, bending down, stared into her face and chuckled. She smelt the stale fumes of whisky, and drew her own conclusions as to the reason for those shaking hands.

'So this is the new patient, is it?' he rasped throatily. 'Well, well, well, we must see if we can't cure her. We're used to 'em, eh, Merrick? Docile ones and raving ones. Well, well, well, this doesn't look as if she'd need a strait jacket or a padded room, but you never can tell. Some of the quietest prove to be the most dangerous.'

He chuckled again and Celia felt her skin grow cold. What was this man, addressed as doctor talking about — padded rooms — strait jackets —

And then like a flash she understood. She had been brought to a private mental home!

12

The Shadow Man

Something of the horror that swept over her must have shown in Celia's eyes, for the horrible old man shook with silent laughter.

'You needn't be frightened, my dear,' he said. His mouth twisted into a leer. 'You needn't be frightened at all. We'll look after you, eh, Merrick?'

'Not so much of the Merrick,' growled that individual.

'What does it matter?' said the bald-headed man impatiently. 'She'll never be able to give you away, or me either.'

He shuffled over to a side table, and picking up a half empty bottle of whisky poured himself nearly a tumbler full of neat spirit.

'Don't you think you'd better leave that stuff alone?' said Merrick, as he raised the glass to his lips and gulped down a good portion of the contents.

'Why should I?' retorted the doctor. 'It's good stuff, and it has no more effect on me than water.'

'All the same, I wouldn't take too much,' warned Merrick.

'You mind your own business,' snarled the other. 'When I want your advice I'll ask for it. You attend to your own job and leave me to attend to mine.'

He finished his drink and set down the empty glass. Merrick shrugged his shoulders.

'Do you want me to leave the girl here?' he asked.

The bald head negatived the question.

'No,' replied the doctor. 'Untie her, and Mrs. Crow can take her to her room.'

Merrick opened his mouth to say something further, changed his mind, and taking a clasp knife from his pocket slashed through the cords at Celia's wrists and ankles.

'There we are! There we are!' cried the doctor cheerfully, as Merrick also removed the gag. 'Now, that's much more comfortable, isn't it? I'm sure it is. You'd like a cup of tea, wouldn't you? Of course you would!'

Without waiting for Celia to reply he shuffled over to the door.

'Hi — you,' he called. 'Bring some tea, and look sharp about it!'

Celia sat up, rubbing her cramped limbs.

'Why have I been brought to this horrible place?' she demanded.

The bald-headed man leered down at her.

'Because you've got to be taken care of,' he said. 'It's not safe for you to be left on your own. You suffer from delusions — '

'I do nothing of the kind,' cried the girl indignantly. 'You're talking nonsense! I've been brought here by a trick.'

'That's one of your delusions,' said the doctor, shaking his head sadly. 'They all have 'em. Some hear voices, and some are always followed about by a black dog — '

'Are you suggesting that I'm mad?' said Celia angrily.

'No, certainly not,' replied the bald-headed man soothingly. 'Not mad, but shall we say, mentally unhinged. It was considered unsafe to leave you at large in case you followed in the footsteps of your father. You see, this slight derangement runs in your family — '

'I never heard anything so ridiculous!' exclaimed the girl, her fear becoming swallowed up by annoyance. 'I insist on being taken home at once!'

'Uncontrollable temper,' murmured the doctor. 'A bad sign.'

'Do you hear me?' cried Celia. 'I insist — '

'It's not a bit of good you insisting on anything,' broke in Merrick. 'Here you are and here you're going to stop, so get that into your head as soon as possible.'

'But you can't keep me here against my will,' began the girl.

'Can't we?' The bald-headed man gave one of his inward chuckles. 'Can't we? My dear young lady. We have kept people here in a much worse state than you are in. There's a room upstairs with padded walls and barred windows. You couldn't get out of that however much you tried. And then we have a strait jacket, a most uncomfortable thing to wear, but, believe me, very effective.'

He didn't raise his voice. He spoke rather like a school teacher to a pupil, but the girl sensed the malignity behind the even tone, and shivered. This vulture-like creature would take a delight in inflicting physical pain, and no amount of pleading would turn him from his purpose. Before she could say anything more the thin-faced, bedraggled woman came in with a cup of tea.

''Ere you are,' she said, thrusting it into Celia's hand, and the girl took it in silence.

The cup was thick and the tea was strong and oversweetened, but the girl drank it gratefully, for her head was still aching from the effects of the drug.

'Have you prepared Miss Lamont's room?' snapped the bald-headed man, and the woman nodded.

'Yes, it's ready,' she replied sullenly.

'Good!' He rubbed his dirty hands together. 'Then as soon as you've finished your tea my dear, Mrs. Crow will take you to your room. I'm sure that you will like a rest.'

Celia looked at him, but made no reply. It was useless talking and she decided that she would not give this drink-sodden creature the pleasure of appearing frightened. She was frightened — terribly frightened, but she wasn't going to show it if she could help it. Neither would she give either of them the satisfaction of arguing. Her best course, since in any case it would make no difference, was to remain silent.

She set down her cup and rose to her feet.

'I'm ready,' she said.

'Come on then,' said the woman, and turning, led the way out into the dingy hall.

The bald-headed man's voice called after them:

'If you feel hungry, my dear, ask Mrs. Crow for what you want.'

The woman mounted the staircase to the bare landing and, taking a bunch of keys from her pocket, unlocked a door on the right. Without a word she stood aside and jerked her head towards the room beyond as an indication for Celia to enter.

The girl did so, looking about her

curiously to see what sort of place had been allotted to her.

She saw a small, almost square room, none too clean, and containing very little furniture.

A strip of threadbare carpet covered the bare boards, and against one wall stood a narrow truckle-bed. One corner was occupied by a rickety washstand, with a tin basin and ewer. A round table and two plain cane-seated chairs completed the contents of the room. The window, its grimy panes protected by stout bars of iron, apparently overlooked the back of the house, for from it Celia caught a glimpse of the refuse-strewn yard through which they had come.

'Think you'll like it?' said Mrs. Crow, with a sneer, watching her from the doorway. 'Well, whether you like it or not you'd better make the best of it. You'll be 'ere fer many a long day, I can tell yer.'

She turned and went out, shutting the door behind her. Celia heard the key turn in the lock, and the steps of the woman go stumbling down the stairs.

For some time she stood still, trying to

persuade her brain to work naturally. The whole incidents from the time she had left the house in Park Road that morning up to the present seemed like the distorted imaginings conjured up by a nightmare, and yet they were real enough. The room with its old and rickety furniture, the house, the horrible old man — they were no figments of the imagination, but solid and substantial.

Vaguely there came to her the recollection of some words of Merrick as he had greeted Mrs. Crow.

'Is the Boss here yet?' and the woman's reply: 'He's in with the doctor.'

Who was the Boss? Was he the person responsible for her having been brought to this place?

There had been nobody in with the doctor when she had been brought in. Who, then, was this mysterious individual who had been mentioned but remained invisible?

She felt dazed and sick. Her head ached dully, and her eyes were hot and tired. Looking round she saw a towel hanging up on a hook behind the door, and going over to the washstand she poured out some water into the basin and bathed her face and hands.

When she had dried them on the towel she felt a little better. The atmosphere of the room was stuffy and heavy, and she went to the window and tried to open it, but she found that several screws had been driven through the sash into the frame, and that it was immovable. Short of breaking the glass there was no way of admitting fresh air. She was looking out into the dreary yard when she heard the sound of a motor engine, and presently the cab came into her field of vision. It crossed the yard and disappeared through the gate.

Merrick then had apparently gone. She concluded that he had finished his part of the business, and the rest was in the hands of the bald-headed doctor and the other man. The other man? This other man worried her. She would have found it difficult to explain why, but the thought of him filled her with an unaccountable fear. She tried to tell herself that whatever he was like he couldn't be worse than the doctor, but it was useless. She supposed it was that peculiar inherent fear of the unknown which is such a strong characteristic of everybody, old and young.

She sat down wearily on one side of the bed, and somehow she must have dropped asleep, for the next thing she knew was that somebody was shaking her by the shoulder, and that a brilliant light was shining in her eyes.

She sat up with a jerk and a stifled cry, blinking into the flame of a candle held in the hand of the woman, Mrs. Crow.

'Bin asleep, 'ave yer?' growled the woman. 'Nice ter be some people, it is. 'Ere yer are, I've brought yer some food.'

She pointed to a tray containing some water and thickly-cut sandwiches which she had set upon a table.

Celia got up immediately.

'Who else is in the house besides you and the doctor?' she asked.

Mrs. Crow gave her a queer look — a half-frightened, half-angry expression that made her thin, unpleasant face even more unpleasant.

'Who told yer there was anyone else?' she demanded crossly.

154

'You did,' said the girl, inspecting the tray of food. 'You told Merrick that somebody called the Boss was in with the doctor.'

'I'm not supposed to answer questions,' snapped Mrs. Crow. 'You'll see what you'll see if you live long enough. Eat yer food and if yer want anything more stamp on the floor.'

She went out and again Celia heard the key click in the lock.

Quite suddenly she discovered that she was ravenously hungry, and when she had eaten the beef sandwiches she felt better. Her long sleep had refreshed her, and her brain felt clearer and more able to cope with the situation.

That she was in a certain amount of danger she was convinced, and she was equally convinced that the danger did not lie with Mrs. Crow or the doctor. It lay with that unknown man whom Merrick had called the Boss.

He was the person to be feared, for he was the instigator — the hand that pulled the strings, the mind that planned.

She tried vainly to find some reason for

all the things that had happened during the past twenty-four hours. Why had her brother been taken to their old house and killed? Who had attacked Doris the maid, and made such a thorough search of the house? And above all, why had she herself been brought to this place and kept a prisoner? What lay behind all this? What was the object?

In the dim flickering light of the candle she sat racking her brains, but all to no purpose. She realised that in some way this affair was connected with the death of her father, but how, was completely beyond her.

Presently she found herself shivering. The room was cold, since no preparations had been made for heating and she fetched a blanket from the bed and wrapped it round her shoulders. The house was very still. Outside it had begun to rain, and she could hear the drip, drip of the water from a broken gutter. And then suddenly the silence was shattered by a banging door from somewhere below, and, listening, she heard steps mounting the stairs.

They drew nearer, came along the

landing, and paused outside her door. There was the rattle of a bunch of keys, the click as the lock turned, and then the door began to open slowly.

Celia, her eyes fixed on that slowly moving door, felt a wave of increasing terror sweep over her. Wider and wider it swung until where it had been was nothing but an oblong piece of blackness. With wide eyes she stared at that menacing darkness, wondering what was coming in — and then she saw!

Out of the cavern of black came a tall figure — the figure of a man that grew clearer as it advanced into the feeble rays from the candle. He was dressed in black from head to foot, and his face was covered by a handkerchief that concealed mouth and nose and chin.

Just inside the doorway he stopped, and his eyes, visible above the obscuring mask, regarded her steadily.

'I want you, Celia Lamont,' he said, and his voice was high, squeaky and unnatural.

Celia felt her throat go suddenly dry and parched. There was something terrifying in that tall, thin figure — that high-pitched inhuman voice.

For a moment after he had spoken he stood motionless, and then he took a step towards her. At the movement the muscles of her throat loosened and she screamed.

13

Sentence of Death

Philip Quest received one of the biggest shocks of his career when he learned from Doris that Celia Lamont had been spirited away by a trick.

Rejoining Lester in the waiting car he briefly explained to his partner this fresh and unexpected development.

'There's something very big behind this business,' he ended gravely. 'Something very big indeed.'

He cut short the questions the other put to him and drove to the police station. There they found Davidson warming himself before the fire in the charge room. The stout Inspector listened in startled amazement to Quest's news.

'This is incredible, Mr. Quest,' he ejaculated. 'What in the world do they want with the girl?'

'I haven't the least idea, Davidson,' said

Quest. 'But I believe she is in very great danger. We must do everything we can to find her.'

Davidson frowned.

'That's not going to be so easy,' he muttered. 'The servant didn't happen to notice the number of that taxi, I suppose?'

The detective shook his head.

'That makes it worse,' went on the Inspector. 'These people couldn't have chosen a better vehicle than a taxi. It's not like a private car that could be traced by its make and colour. There are so many taxis about that nobody looks at them twice. Anyhow, we'll do our best.'

He went into his office and picked up the telephone.

Fifteen minutes the telephone wires were humming, carrying the news to every police station in the country with a description of the girl and instructions to look out for her. It was a forlorn hope, and nobody knew it better than Quest and Davidson, but it was all they could do for the moment.

'Where have you put Harding?' asked

the detective when the Inspector had finished his telephoning.

'In one of the cells,' answered Davidson. 'Do you want to see him?'

'Yes,' said Quest, 'I think he ought to know about the disappearance of Miss Lamont. It might have the effect of loosening his tongue.'

He found Harding sitting on the plank bed smoking a cigarette. He looked up as they entered and raised his eyebrows.

'Come to do some more questioning?' he enquired. 'Well, let me tell you, you are wasting your time. If you keep me here till doomsday I've got nothing more to tell you.'

'I haven't come to question you,' said Quest. 'I've come to give you a piece of information. Miss Lamont has been kidnapped!'

Harding leapt to his feet, his face white, and the cigarette fell to the floor with a little shower of sparks.

'That's a lie!' he cried harshly. 'You're making it up to try and trick me — '

'I'm doing nothing of the sort,' snapped the detective. 'I'm telling you the truth.'

161

He related what had occurred, and Harding listened, his face becoming drawn and haggard as Quest proceeded.

'Good Heavens, how awful!' he exclaimed when the detective had finished. 'What are you going to do? You must do something.'

'We have done all we can for the moment,' broke in Quest. 'I was hoping that you would be able to help us.'

'I — I — how can I help you?' asked Harding.

'You know who is at the bottom of this business,' said the detective. 'You know who killed Richard Lamont and why. Tell us what you know and you will be helping us more than you realise.'

Harding was silent. His mouth was compressed into a thin line, and his brows were so tightly knitted that they almost obscured his eyes. A minute passed — two, and then, suddenly making up his mind, he raised his head.

'Very well,' he said. 'Under the circumstances I will tell you all I know.'

'I think you're sensible,' said Philip Quest. 'And be as brief as possible. Time is precious; a few minutes either way may mean the difference between Miss Lamont's life — and death!'

★   ★   ★

'You can scream as much as you like,' said the shadowy figure in that horrible high-pitched squeak. 'Nobody will hear you.'

Celia's momentary panic subsided. Her fear had by no means abated, but she realised the futility of giving way to it.

Clenching her teeth tightly she crouched back against the bed, keeping her eyes fixed on the half-masked face.

The man nodded approvingly.

'That's right — keep calm,' he said. 'It will be much better for you if you do.'

'What do you want? Who are you?' she gasped with dry lips.

He shrugged his shoulders.

'Never mind who I am,' he answered. 'That doesn't concern you in the least. What I want is a different matter — that does concern you. I want you to come downstairs with me.'

'What for?' she asked. 'What are you going to do with me?'

'At present nothing,' said the shadow-man. 'Except ask you a few questions. If you answer them truthfully then we'll see what can be done with you.'

Something in the way he uttered the last part of his remark sent a cold shiver down her back. But she conquered her fear and answered him calmly.

'What questions?' she demanded.

'That you will find out when we ask them,' he said. 'Come along.'

He turned towards the black oblong of the doorway. For the fraction of a second she hesitated, and then, realising the uselessness of refusing, followed him out of the room. The landing and the staircase were in pitch darkness, but he took her by the arm and led her. Once, going down the stairs, she stumbled and would have fallen but for his supporting hand.

The door of the room into which she had been taken when Merrick first brought her to the house stood half open, sending a fan-shaped wedge of light spreading across the hall. Towards this the

164

shadow-man made his way, kicked the door wide, and pushed her into the room beyond.

The bald-headed old doctor was standing in front of the fireplace clad in a shabby dressing-gown, and the girl saw at once that he had been drinking heavily.

'Hello, my dear,' he greeted jovially. 'Come down to join us, eh? That's right — that's right — merry little party.'

'Shut up, Rule,' hissed the masked man angrily. 'You've been at that whisky again. I told you to leave it alone.'

'Only a spot, my dear fellow,' said Doctor Rule with a leer. 'Only a spot. This business is thirsty work — besides, I can always think better when I've had a spot.'

'I don't want you to think,' snapped the other. 'I'll do all the thinking that's necessary. You were comparatively sober this morning. Why couldn't you keep like it?'

'I'm com — com — er — quite sober now,' insisted the doctor. 'You can't make me drunk. There isn't enough drink in the world to make me drunk. Do you know that, my dear' — he turned his bloodshot eyes towards Celia — 'not enough drink in the world. But when this business is over and I've got the money that's coming to me I'm going to try to find enough. I'm going — '

'You're going to be quiet, you fool!' snarled the shadow-man threateningly. 'By Heaven, if I'd known you were going to get like this — ' He left the sentence unfinished and gripped the bald-headed man's arm. 'Pull yourself together, will you?'

The other's eyes met his, read the fury in their cold depths, and something of the colour went from his vulture-like face.

'I'm sorry,' he muttered. 'I'm all right really — quite all right, my dear fellow.'

'Well, then, don't make a fool of yourself,' said the masked man. 'Sit down, Miss Lamont, and we will get to business.'

The girl sat down in silence, her heart cold with dread.

'Now,' said the man in black, still speaking in the forced, unnatural voice he had used all the time, 'you have in your possession two veils that your father gave you before his death.'

She gave a little gasp of comprehension. So that was what they were after, was it? He was quick to notice the half-stifled exclamation, and went on quickly:

'I see that there is no need for me to explain further. You understand to what I refer?'

She nodded.

'Well,' he continued, 'those veils were not your father's property to give you. They belong to — well, to friends of mine and those friends want them. Your house was searched to find them, but they couldn't be found, so we have brought you here to tell us where they are.'

He stopped and waited for her to speak. She was such a long time that he grew impatient.

'Come!' he said. 'It's a simple thing I'm asking — merely that you hand over to me two veils which you have in your possession.'

'I can't — ' she began huskily.

'Why not?' he interrupted harshly.

'Because I haven't got them,' she answered.

'But you can tell us where they are?' he insisted.

'Oh, yes, I can do that,' she replied, and his tense attitude relaxed.

'That's the same thing,' he said. 'Now, where are they?'

'I gave them to Mr. Philip Quest,' she answered simply.

The effect of her remark was startling. The bald-headed doctor uttered a lurid oath. The masked man took a step forward, his hands clenched.

'You — gave — them — to — Philip Quest?' he hissed, separately articulating each word.

'Yes,' she said steadily.

'She's lying!' exclaimed Doctor Rule. 'She's lying — hoping to bluff us.'

'I'm not lying, and I'm not trying to bluff you,' said Celia. 'I gave those veils to Mr. Quest.'

'Why?' asked the man in black sharply.

'Because he asked me for them,' said Celia.

'How did he know anything about

them?' cried the doctor. 'How did he know they ever existed? Tell us that?'

Celia shot him a contemptuous glance.

'He knew because I told him,' she said. 'I told him my father had given them to me before he died, and he was interested — '

'Is that all you told him?' broke in the man in the mask.

'What do you mean?' asked the girl.

'I mean, did you tell him anything else,' he answered. 'Did you tell him what they were for, for instance?'

'As I don't know what they were for, I couldn't, very well — could I?' she retorted.

'Is that true?' said the doctor. 'Don't you know what they're for?'

'Since you seem to think that everything I say is a lie, it doesn't appear much good answering that,' said Celia with a calmness she was far from feeling. 'But all the same, I don't.'

'Didn't your father tell you?' asked the other, eyeing her keenly.

She shook her head.

'My father told me nothing,' she

replied. 'I can't help whether you believe me or not, but it's true.'

There was a moment's silence, broken at length by the bald-headed man.

'I don't believe her,' he said, shaking his massive head. 'She's only saying that to bluff us.'

'I don't agree with you,' said the other. 'I believe that the girl is speaking the truth. After all, when you come to think of it, it's hardly likely that Lamont would have told her — or anyone, for that matter.'

'But his own daughter!' protested Rule.

'He didn't tell the son, did he?' came the swift reply. 'So why should he tell the daughter?'

'Well, whether she's telling the truth or not,' muttered the bald-headed man, 'the thing is: how are we going to get hold of those veils?'

'Yes, that's the question.' The masked man nodded. 'We'll have to go after Quest, that's all. There's nothing else for it.'

Doctor Rule made a wry grimace.

'That's going to be difficult,' he said.

170

'Besides being darned risky.'

'Risky or difficult, it's got to be done!' snapped the other. 'We shall have to think it over and decide on a plan. Has Merrick come back?'

'Yes, he's out in the kitchen with Mrs. Crow,' answered the doctor.

'Call him,' said the shadow-man tersely.

Doctor Rule went over to the door and shouted.

'What do you want Merrick for?' he asked, coming back and taking up his stand once more in front of the fire.

'He can take the girl upstairs while we decide what's to be done,' was the reply.

There was the sound of feet in the passage, and Merrick came in. He looked enquiringly from one to the other.

'Take Miss Lamont back to her room and lock her in,' ordered the masked man. 'Here are the keys!' He tossed them over and Merrick deftly caught them. 'When you've done that come back here.'

'Right you are,' said Merrick. 'Come on!'

He turned to the girl and jerked his

head towards the door.

Celia rose with something like relief. She would be glad to get out of that overheated room, with its atmosphere of stale spirits — glad to get away from the vulture-faced doctor and his more sinister companion.

'Don't go to bed,' said the latter, as she followed Merrick to the door. 'I shall want you again.'

She made no reply, but passed on into the darkness of the hall. As she reached the foot of the stairs she heard Dr. Rule say, in a low voice:

'What are you going to do with her?'

'She'll have to die,' came the high-pitched squeaky voice.

Celia felt herself swaying, and clutched the banisters for support.

She had heard her own death sentence!

14

Harding's Story

James Harding looked at Philip Quest and there was horror in his eyes.

'Do you really think it's as serious as all that?' he asked huskily.

'I do,' replied the detective shortly. 'These people have already committed two murders, which should show that they are desperate. They won't stick at a third if it suits their purpose.'

Harding lit a fresh cigarette with a shaking hand.

'I'll tell you everything I know,' he said. 'But I'm afraid it's not going to help you as much as you think.' He paused for the fraction of a second, as though considering how to begin. 'You were quite right,' he went on, 'when you thought that I had learned something in Johannesburg about Lamont. I did. The reason I didn't tell Celia and refused to tell you was because it wasn't particularly to his credit.'

'I was under the impression that that was the reason,' murmured Quest. 'Go on.'

'Lamont, as you probably know, was the chief-engineer of the Blue Clay diamond mine, owned by the De Greers,' continued Harding. 'When he came to England this last time and told his daughter that he had retired he was lying. He didn't retire. He was sacked. I learned all this from the manager of the mine, Souza, and I also learned the reason.'

He took a long pull at the cigarette and exhaled the smoke slowly.

'I don't know whether or not you know anything about diamond mining,' he said, 'but out there it is a criminal offence to buy diamonds, under the I.D.B. laws. The penalty is a very severe one — at least two years on the Breakwater at Cape Town.'

Philip Quest nodded.

'I know all that,' he answered.

'Well, then you can understand that every precaution is exercised to ensure that the native workmen cannot steal any stones,' said Harding. 'After coming out of the mine they are put into a compound and searched, and this is done with a thoroughness that makes it impossible for them to conceal anything on their persons. There is only one point in the intricate chain of operations that the rough diamonds pass through before they finally reach the valuing office, where theft would be possible, and that is in the sorting rooms. For this reason the sorters are always white men, picked very carefully with reference to their honesty. I am being as brief as possible, but I must tell you this in order to make what follows clear.'

Again he inhaled deeply.

'Two of these sorters, a man named Bishop and another named Cowley, entered into a conspiracy to steal some of the diamonds that passed through their hands. The only difficulty they had to overcome was the rigid searching that each sorter had to undergo on entering and leaving the sorting room, and this, with the assistance of Lamont, they did overcome. How they persuaded a man like Lamont to have anything to do with barefaced robbery I don't know. Souza suggested that they had managed to have some hold over him.

'Apparently for some time Lamont had been gambling heavily and was seriously in debt, so this is the most likely explanation. However, they did rope him into the scheme, which was a simple one. In the sorting room the diamond-bearing gravel is brought in, a sieveful at a time, and dumped on tables covered with iron plates, and the sorter scrapes a little of it towards him with a sheet of zinc. He rapidly passes the grains under review, picks out the diamonds and puts them in a small tin box in front of him. Now, although each sorter is thoroughly searched on entering and leaving the sorting room, he is left entirely to himself in the room, the argument being that it would be useless for him to steal any diamonds because of the impossibility of getting away with them.

'As I said, Bishop and Cowley solved this problem. With the aid of small pieces of chewing gum they stuck the diamonds they filched under the sorting room table and left them to be collected by Lamont when the day's work was over; for Lamont, being chief engineer, had access to all the rooms, and was allowed to pass in and out unmolested, particularly since at that time of the day all the valuable diamond-bearing gravel was locked in the huge safe provided for the purpose.'

'H'm, a variation of the old jeweller's shop fraud,' remarked Philip Quest who had been listening to Harding with intense interest. 'That's no doubt where they got the idea.'

Harding nodded.

'Well, this pilfering went on for nearly a year,' he said, 'and during that time an enormous quantity of diamonds must have passed into the hands of Lamont. These were, of course, rough stones, and, owing to the I.D.B. laws, could not be sold out there. What arrangements had been come to between the three as to how the diamonds were to be eventually disposed of I don't know. The whole scheme was discovered before that could be put into practice. Cowley and Bishop were caught and sentenced to two years on the Breakwater. At their trial they had refused to state how they had managed to get the diamonds out of the sorting room or where the stones had been hidden. Souza, however, who had discovered the fraud, had his own suspicions concerning Lamont, and Lamont received his notice. He, as you know, came home, presumably bringing the diamonds with him, and that's all I know.'

Quest frowned.

'It carries us a step further, anyhow,' he said. 'We know who is at the bottom of this business — Bishop and Cowley.'

'But they would still be serving their sentence, Mr. Quest,' put in Davidson. 'If they got two years — '

'Bishop died as the result of an accident on the Breakwater,' said Harding, 'and Cowley escaped.'

'Why,' said Quest, 'did Souza come to England, and why did he take Richard Lamont to that empty house?'

'He came to England partly on a holiday and partly on business,' answered Harding. 'The business was in connection with the stolen diamonds. From what he told me — '

He broke off as a constable appeared at the door of the cell.

'The desk-sergeant would like you to come up, sir,' said the policeman, addressing Inspector Davidson. 'There's a taxi driver just come who's had his cab stolen — '

Quest looked round sharply.

'When was it stolen?' he asked.

'Some time this morning, he says, sir,' answered the constable.

'Then it's the cab that was used to carry off Miss Lamont,' snapped Quest. 'We'd better see this man at once, Davidson. From him we can get the number of the cab, and possibly be able to trace it.'

'Have I got to remain here?' asked Harding. 'Can't I come and help?'

Quest looked at the Inspector.

'I don't think there's any need to keep Mr. Harding here now, is there?' he asked.

Davidson pursed his lips dubiously.

'Well, we've had no confirmation of this

story of his — ' he began heavily.

'Good Heavens, you don't think I'd lie at a time like this, do you?' said Harding. 'I only told you what I knew because Celia was in danger. Anyway, I give you my word I won't run away, or anything, only let me be in it. I shall go crazy if I'm left here without knowing what's going on.'

Davidson opened his mouth to reply, caught Quest's eye, and nodded.

'All right,' he said grudgingly. 'Only I shall have to insist that you stay with us all the time. You can't go off by yourself.'

'I don't want to,' said Harding. 'I just want to know what's happening — that's all.'

'Now let us go and see the taxi-driver,' said Quest impatiently, and Davidson signed to the constable.

They left the cell and followed the policeman up to the charge room.

By the sergeant's desk stood a large, fat man enveloped in a massive overcoat. His face was very red, shot here and there with splashes of purple. He carried his hat in his hand, revealing an almost completely bald head, the shining surface of which was lightly streaked with ginger hair well plastered down. A ragged moustache of the same fiery hue adorned his long upper lip. He turned and surveyed the newcomers through a pair of light blue watery eyes.

'Here is Inspector Davidson,' remarked the desk sergeant, jerking his pen towards that stout official. 'You can tell him all about it.'

The taxi-driver, whose name turned out to be Will Jinks, told Davidson all about it. Shorn of his many picturesque additions to the English in the form of lurid oaths, his story was a brief one. The cab was his own property, and he had been out on early duty in West Hill. There was, it appeared, an ample opportunity for picking up a business gentleman or two and running them to the station. The morning being cold he had, after dropping his third fare at the station, gone to a coffee shop for a cup of coffee. It was against the regulations to leave the cab unattended in the street outside the shop, so he ran it into a side turning close by where it could be left.

When he had finished his coffee and gone back for the cab it wasn't there.

He had concluded that one of his friends had played a trick on him — they were fond of practical joking and had done the same sort of thing once before. On that occasion he had taken the cab up to the rank and left it there, and there had been much laughter at his — Will Jinks' — expense.

He had walked up to the rank, found his friends, but no cab.

Apparently it had taken them a long time to convince him that they were not responsible for the disappearance of the cab, but when they had Mr. Jinks had come straight to the police station.

Inspector Davidson listened in silence to the cabman's story, and when he had finished, breathless and perspiring, he turned to the desk sergeant.

'Have you taken particulars of the make and the number?' he asked.

'Yes, sir,' The sergeant turned to his desk and read out in the monotonous voice he assumed for such occasions:

'Green painted Renault, 1932 model,

registration number LX 2789, hackney carriage, registration number IO 786. Left rear mudguard badly bent. Patched tyre on right front wheel.'

'Green painted Renault, number LX 2789,' repeated the Inspector. 'H'm, all right, Mr. Jinks, we'll send out a call straight away, and do our best to find your cab. As soon as we have any news we'll communicate with you.'

'You've got my address, ain't yer?' said Mr. Jinks, looking at the stolid desk sergeant, and that worthy nodded.

''E's got it,' he said unnecessarily. 'I'll wait an' 'ear from yer then.'

He replaced the greasy cap on his head and walked over to the door.

'Yer'll get a move on, won't yer?' he remarked, pausing on the threshold. 'The old cab's me livin' an' I ain't made so much lately that I can afford ter sit back an' take it easy, like.'

'You can depend upon it that we shall be as prompt as we can,' said Inspector Davidson.

'Awlright, then, I'll 'ope ter 'ear from yer soon,' said Mr. Jinks. 'So long.'

He went out, closing the door behind him.

'There's no doubt,' said Davidson, 'that Jinks' cab is the one we're after. Apart from the fact that it would be too great a coincidence, taxicabs are rarely stolen for gain. They're too difficult to get rid of.'

'Oh, that's the cab right enough,' agreed Quest. 'The question is, can we trace it? If we can we ought to be able to find out where Miss Lamont has been taken.'

'I'll put the description over the wires at once,' said the Inspector, and hurried into his private office.

'It's pretty well a forlorn hope, I should think,' muttered Harding despondently. 'Taxis are pretty common nowadays. Nobody is likely to have noticed this particular one.'

'There's always the chance that a policeman on point duty may have noticed and remembered the number,' answered Quest. 'If that should have occurred in this case we shall know the direction in which the cab containing Miss Lamont was travelling.'

But apparently no policeman on point duty had noticed the number, or if he had, had not remembered it, for no reply came through in answer to the all-stations call that Davidson had sent out.

The afternoon wore on and merged into evening. By six o'clock Philip Quest was beginning to show obvious signs of the strain. His face had grown very stern.

He had refused to leave the station, even for lunch, and sandwiches had been sent in. Huddled up in a chair in front of the charge room fire he smoked cigarette after cigarette and racked his brains to think of some plan that would enable them to trace Celia Lamont. But he could devise nothing. There was nothing that could be done except wait. They had not the slightest idea in which direction the girl had been taken, and she might at that moment be anywhere in England. Their only hope lay in the tracing of the stolen taxi.

Harding was in a worse state than Quest. Unable to remain still, he raced up and down till the desk sergeant began to feel dizzy.

The strain had almost reached breaking point when Mr. Wilkins, carrying out his avowed intention, arrived at the police station and exploded his bombshell in their midst.

He came in quietly and rather nervously, but the first words he uttered riveted everybody's attention on him.

'I wants ter see the feller what's in charge of this Lamont murder job,' he said approaching the desk. 'I've got some information.'

The desk sergeant sat up alertly. Philip Quest sprang to his feet. Harding ceased his restless pacing, stopped dead and stared at Mr. Wilkins as though he had been a ghost. Lester removed his elbow from the mantelpiece against which he had been leaning and took a step forward.

'That will be Inspector Davidson,' said the desk sergeant, recovering his official immobility. 'He's in his office. I'll tell him.'

'I'll tell him,' said Lester, and crossed the floor towards Davidson's tiny room.

Mr. Wilkins swelled visibly with importance. He had never created such a sensation before in his life. What a yarn this would make to tell his friends at the Crown and Anchor. He wished they were there to see him at the moment, the centre of attraction — the star turn. But particularly he wished that Emily could have been there. She might treat him with a little more respect after that. He leaned against the desk with an easy, confident air and waited.

Inspector Davidson came hurrying out of his office, followed by Lester.

'You want to see me about the Lamont murder?' he asked, and Mr. Wilkins nodded.

'Yus,' he answered. 'An' about my lodger. 'E's mixed up in it some'ow.'

'Let me have your name and address, please,' said Davidson, and signed to the sergeant, who dipped his pen in the ink expectantly.

'Bert Wilkins,' said Mr. Wilkins grandly, '14, Tate Street.'

The desk sergeant entered it in his book.

'Now, Mr. Wilkins,' said the stout Inspector, 'we shall be very pleased to hear what you have to tell us.'

Mr. Wilkins was very pleased to tell them, and as a final gesture produced from his pocket a charred scrap of paper.

'There yer are!' he said triumphantly. 'There yer are! You can see fer yerself.'

Davidson looked at it, read the words on the scorched surface, uttered an exclamation, and handed it to Philip Quest.

There were seven words in all, and the detective's eyes gleamed as he saw them.

' — Tree Avenue — house is empty — Lamont will — '

'This is a most important clue!' he exclaimed. 'You say your lodger Merrick is out at present?'

'That's right,' agreed Mr. Wilkins.

'Then I think we'll come back with you,' said Quest, 'and have a look at his room. There may be something there that will give us a clue to his present whereabouts.' He turned to Harding. 'I have an idea that if we can find this man Merrick we shall also find Celia Lamont.'

15

The Marked Map

Philip Quest took Lester with him to Tate Street, leaving Harding and Inspector Davidson at the station to await any possible news that might come through.

It was raining heavily when they turned the car into the narrow street and brought it to a halt outside number 14.

Mr. Wilkins opened the door with his latchkey and ushered them into the dark hall.

'Hi, Emily!' he called. 'Bring a light, will yer — and look sharp. I've got two gents with me.'

Quest heard a startled exclamation from somewhere in the regions beyond the end of the passage, and presently a stout little woman clad in a voluminous apron appeared, carrying a candle.

'This 'ere's Mr. Philip Quest, the detective,' greeted Mr. Wilkins proudly, beaming in the reflected glory of the famous name. 'Yer've 'eard about 'im, of course. 'E wants ter 'ave a look at that bloke's room.'

Mrs. Wilkins looked nervous and not a little alarmed.

'I 'ope there ain't going ter be no trouble,' she said in a slightly-scared voice.

'I don't think you need have any fear, Mrs. Wilkins,' said Quest reassuringly. 'Both you and your husband have acted in a most praiseworthy way and deserve every thanks. I will personally promise you that every effort will be made to avoid you suffering any unpleasantness.'

'That's very kind of you, I'm sure, sir,' said Mrs. Wilkins, still a little doubtfully. 'Did yer want to go up to Mr. Merrick's room now, sir?'

'Yes, please,' said Quest. 'He is, of course, still out, I presume?'

'Oh, yes, sir. 'E's still out,' said Mrs. Wilkins beginning to mount the staircase. 'Though of course I couldn't say as to when 'e's likely to come 'ome. 'E might come in at any minute.'

'We shall have to take the risk of that,' said the detective, following close on her heels.

She made no reply, but went up until she reached the door on the top landing that gave access to Merrick's room.

'This is the room, sir,' she said, and opened the door. 'If you'll wait a moment I'll light the gas.'

She disappeared into the semi-darkness with the candle. After a slight delay there was a small 'pop' and the glaring light of an incandescent burner dispersed the gloom.

Philip Quest entered, accompanied by Lester, and glanced round the room. It was very neat and tidy, though poorly furnished.

'That's where I found the bit of paper, sir,' said Mrs. Wilkins, pointing to the empty grate. 'It were among a whole lot of burnt paper.'

Quest nodded, still letting his eyes wander round the small apartment.

'You took the burnt stuff away, I suppose?' he asked.

'I'm afraid I did, sir,' confessed Mrs.

Wilkins; 'but there weren't nothin' else that wasn't burnt, sir.'

'I see.' The detective crossed over to the table and looked over the collection of articles heaped on it.

There was a half empty packet of cigarettes, three partly used boxes of matches, a dirty glass which smelt of whisky, and several newspapers. He picked these up and shook them out in the hope that something might have been concealed in their folds, but there was nothing.

'There's nothing here, anyway,' he remarked to Lester, who stood at his elbow. 'That, I presume, is Merrick's luggage. Perhaps we shall be luckier there.'

He went over to the two suitcases that stood at the foot of the bed. They weren't locked, and in a few seconds he had them open and, with the assistance of Lester, was rummaging among their contents.

Mrs. Wilkins had taken up her position beside her husband in the doorway, and was watching the proceedings with marked interest and curiosity.

One suitcase contained nothing but clothes. Two suits, rather the worse for wear, a pair of flannel trousers and a sports jacket. The other was full of shirts, collars, pyjamas and underclothes. There was nothing in any of the pockets of the suits and nothing among the linen.

'Mr. Merrick is evidently a very careful gentleman,' murmured Quest. 'He evidently takes the precaution of burning everything in the nature of documentary evidence. There's not a scrap of writing to be found anywhere here. Not even an old envelope. I suppose he received some letters while he was here?' he asked addressing Mrs. Wilkins.

''E's 'ad one or two,' answered her husband, determined not to be left out of the proceedings. 'Swanky envelopes they was, too.'

'And he took the precaution of burning them,' said the detective. 'The scrap you found was just bad luck.'

He tumbled the things back in the bags and straightened up.

'Have a look in the wardrobe, Lester,' he said, 'while I tackle this cupboard.'

He crossed to a cupboard in one corner and pulled at the handle.

'Hello, this looks more promising!' he said. 'It's locked!'

'And 'e's taken the key with 'im,' put in Mrs. Wilkins. 'It always used ter be in the lock.'

'Well, if there's anything, it'll be in there,' said Lester. 'Because the wardrobe is as empty as Mother Hubbard's cupboard.'

Quest took a little twisted wire instrument from his pocket and inserted it in the lock. It was an ordinary flimsy affair and it yielded at the first attempt with a click.

The detective repocketed the little instrument and pulled open the door.

At first glance he saw only a partly empty bottle of whisky, several glasses and a corkscrew, and then his eyes fell on a folded object at the back of the shelf, and he took it out. His exclamation brought Lester hurrying over from the wardrobe.

'What is it?' he asked excitedly.

'A great piece of luck,' replied Philip

Quest. 'A motoring map of England, and there's a route marked on it in pencil.'

He spread the map out on to the table and pointed to the thick pencil line that ran across the surface.

'Southwater has been ringed round,' said Lester.

Quest nodded.

'Yes, it's a small place beyond Horsham,' he said, 'and it's ten to one that's where they've taken Celia Lamont.'

He folded up the map and stuffed it into the pocket of his coat.

'Come on,' he said crisply, 'we'll get back to the station.'

He turned to Mr. Wilkins.

'I am extremely grateful for the trouble you have taken,' he said, 'and I will see that you are suitably rewarded. In the meanwhile I think it is only fair to tell you that your lodger is a very dangerous man, and I am taking the precaution of sending a constable up from the station to keep this house under observation and arrest Merrick should he put in an appearance before I get back.'

'Oh, dear,' cried Mrs. Wilkins. 'I knew

there'd be trouble.' And she broke into voluble lamentations which followed them down the stairs as they made hurriedly for the front door.

Ten minutes later they were back in the charge room at the police station, and here news awaited them.

A message had just come through from the Sussex police to say that a taxicab bearing the number LX 2789 had been found abandoned in a lane off the Horsham Road.

'That confirms the route marked on the map,' said Quest. 'Our next step I think is Southwater.'

Harding was all excitement.

'Can I come with you?' he demanded.

'If Inspector Davidson has no objection,' replied Quest, looking at the stout official, and Davidson shrugged his plump shoulders.

'I don't see why not,' he said. 'But what are we going to do when we get to Southwater?'

'Find Celia Lamont first of all,' snapped the detective, 'and arrest Merrick.'

Davidson flushed.

'I know that,' he said crossly. 'I mean how are we going to find out where their bolt-hole is?'

Quest pointed to the map lying open on the sergeant's desk.

'Just outside the circle enclosing Southwater,' he said, 'there's a pencilled dot. I conclude that it marks the site of a house of some sort, and that is where he was making.'

Davidson glanced at the spot and nodded.

'I see what you mean,' he said. 'Well, then, we'd better be going.'

He issued a string of orders and presently joined Quest, Lester and Harding by the waiting car.

Philip Quest had already fixed the map to the dashboard with drawing pins in such a position that it was lit up by the pilot light and taken his place at the wheel, with Lester beside him. Davidson got in the back with Harding and the big car drove away.

The night was very dark, and the rain was falling steadily, but Quest was a skilful driver and despite the skidding surface of the road kept the car at a good speed.

The straggling line of streets and houses soon gave way to open country, and here the needle of the speedometer began to move upwards.

Davidson's huge hands clenched in his pockets and he closed his eyes. Even Lester, who was used to the detective's driving, felt his heart begin to beat a trifle faster as the needle passed forty — forty-five — fifty, and settled steadily at sixty.

But Philip Quest, peering ahead through the semi-circular patch of glass cleaned by the swinging screen-wiper, was as unmoved and calm as if he had been sitting by the fire in his flat. On through the darkness and rain they went, slackening speed only as they passed through a village or town, and picking up again as soon as it had flashed by.

Westerham — Oxted — Edenbridge — East Grinstead. Here they swung off the main road on to a secondary road. The surface was bad and Quest was forced to lessen speed slightly; but even here he kept the needle hovering between the fifty and fifty-five mark.

Horsham!

They passed through the town and were back again on the main road.

'We should be a little less than five miles from Southwater now,' muttered Quest, speaking for the first time. 'According to the points on the map, the house we want is somewhere off the main road this side of the place. I'll go slow, Lester, and you keep a lookout on the left and I'll do the same on the right.'

He dropped the speed to a crawl and allowed the car to move slowly along by the side of the road. They had proceeded thus for about three miles without passing any likely looking turning, when Lester suddenly laid his hand on the detective's arm.

'There's a lane there,' he said. 'It looks as if it might lead to a house.'

Quest brought the car to a halt.

'This is where we proceed on foot,' he remarked, getting out, 'and I think the best thing would be for Lester and me to go on ahead and explore, while you and

Harding wait here in the car. If we've struck the right place we can come back and let you know and decide the next move.'

Davidson agreed but Harding demurred.

'It's going to cause delay,' he said, 'and if Celia's in any danger — '

Quest cut him short quickly.

'We're not certain yet,' he said, 'that this is the place we're looking for. If it is, the four of us are likely enough to make some noise and put the people we're after on their guard. If it isn't two of us can find out and get back quicker than four.'

He took his partner's arm.

'Come on,' he said, before Harding could argue any farther, and they set off down the dark and uninviting lane.

16

The Car in The Lane

The rutted surface was soggy underfoot and they had to move slowly. The swish of the rain as it beat against the hedges on either side struck mournfully on their ears, but it was the only sound that broke the silence of the night. The lane was pitch black and seemingly unending, and once, as it swung unexpectedly round to the right Lester nearly stumbled into a ditch.

'I can't see anything ahead,' he whispered. 'At least, no light or anything that looks like a house.'

'Neither can I,' replied Quest, 'but this must lead somewhere.'

'A ploughed field, I should think,' muttered Lester disgustedly, and stopped as the detective suddenly gripped his arm.

'Look there, to the right,' said the detective softly.

Lester looked, and saw, very faintly, glimmering through a gap in the hedgerow that hemmed them in, a yellow blur.

'That looks as if we were near some sort of a house, anyway,' he answered.

They moved forward again very cautiously and as silently as possible. It was difficult to maintain complete silence, for their footsteps squelched in the rivulets of water that ran down the cart-tracks with which the lane was rutted. The light half seen through the branches was deceptive in that darkness, for after they had proceeded for a considerable distance it seemed as far away as ever. Steadily and unwinkingly it glowed in the blackness, apparently surrounded by nothing, for they could see nothing either above or below or round it. The lane took another curve to the right, not so sharp as the last, and they were just rounding the bend when Quest stopped dead.

'What — ' began Lester, but the detective pressed his arm warningly, and he broke off.

'Look ahead,' whispered Quest, with his lips close to the other's ear. 'Unless

I'm mistaken that's a car standing without lights.'

Lester strained his eyes. He was getting used to the darkness now and was able to make out the dim, bulky shape that Quest's keener eyesight had first seen. There was no doubt that it was a car, and it stood in front of a half-open gate, evidently the entrance to the house from which the light came.

'It's a car right enough,' breathed Lester, and was again stopped, this time by the sound of an opening door from somewhere ahead.

There came the faint mutter of a man's voice and the stumble of footsteps.

Quest crouched back under the dripping hedge, pulling the lad with him. The footsteps came nearer, and then distinctly to their straining ears floated a girl's voice, hoarse and high-pitched with fear.

'Where are you taking me?' it asked.

'You'll see,' came the deep tones of a man's voice in answer.

'That was Celia Lamont,' whispered Quest tensely. 'We've found the right place.'

Lester nodded, his eyes straining to pierce the darkness in front. Now he could make out a darker splash against the background of gloom by the gate; a darker splash that resolved itself into two splashes that moved towards the bulk of the car. The click of an opening door reached his ears and he felt Quest stiffen.

'They're going by car,' said the detective. 'Quickly, go back to Davidson and get our car out of the way. Switch off the lights and run it right into the side of the road, and then follow this car.'

'What about you?' murmured Lester.

'I'm going to stay here and see if I can't learn more of what is happening,' replied Quest. 'Now, quickly,' he added, as the whirr of an electric starter broke the silence, 'off you go or you'll be too late.'

Lester glided away from his side and was lost in the darkness.

Quest heard the engine of the car in front throb to life, accelerate and die down to a rhythmic beat, there came the grating of gears, and the dark shadowy mass began to move. It went forward, backed and went forward again. The driver was evidently trying to turn it in the narrow confines of the lane. Eventually he succeeded, for it began to move towards the place where Quest was crouching. On it came, gathering speed, and as it passed him Quest made up his mind. He could see now that it was a two-seater coupé, and, springing forward he clutched at the back, gripped one of the rear mudguards, and swung himself up on to the sloping cover of the dicky seat.

It was smooth and shiny with the rain, and he had the greatest difficulty in retaining his hold, especially since the car was bumping badly over the ruts in the lane, but he succeeded in wedging his foot against the rear lamp bracket. Thus precariously perched he managed to hang on, but he hoped that he was not in for a long journey. The car negotiated the windings of the lane and came out on the main road. Quest looked around for his own car but could not see it anywhere. Lester then had succeeded in getting it out of the way in time, but it could only have been just in time. It must have been practically by a hair's-breadth. The coupé was making in the direction of Horsham, and Quest wondered where they were bound. Was the girl being taken back to London, and, if so, for what reason? Why, if they were taking her back now, had they ever brought her here at all?

He came to the conclusion that they were not taking her back to London, but for some reason were taking her to another place. Perhaps Merrick had been informed of his — Quest's — visit to Tate Street, and was taking precautions.

The detective smiled grimly. If that were so he had acted too late. He looked back to see if he could see Lester and the other car following, but there was no sign of it. If there at all it was running without lights, and the steadily falling rain made visibility difficult.

The coupé was now moving at a high speed, and Quest was wondering how long they were going to keep this up, when it slowed, turned into a side track and, a hundred yards further on, came to a halt. The engine was stopped, and Quest, slipping quickly from the back, took up his position behind an adjacent tree trunk. The car had been stopped on the fringe of a wood, but so far as he could see there was no sign of a house or habitation of any kind. Why, then, had it stopped here?

The door of the coupé was opened and the girl got out, followed instantly by the man. Quest could not see him sufficiently well to see what he looked like. He caught the girl by the arm and dragged her towards the wood, and as they vanished into the gloom of the trees Quest followed. As he did so he thought he heard the purring of a car engine faintly, and, looking back, caught a momentary glimpse of a light back along the road he had come. It only flashed for a second and was gone, but he guessed that it came from Lester and the others with the car.

He reached the wood and peered into its dark depths. He could see nothing, but from somewhere ahead came the sound of breaking twigs under the pressure of feet, and he followed the sound. Presently he heard the murmur of voices — the girl's and the man's — a short silence, and then a loud oath and the noise of flying feet coming towards him.

'Darn you, come here!' snarled the man's voice, and further lumbering steps were added to the others.

Quest stopped, dodging behind a tree. He guessed what had happened from the sounds. Celia Lamont had broken free from her captor and was making an effort to escape. The detective thought quickly. Should he intervene now and help the girl, or wait a little longer? If he made his presence known now there was every chance that he would lose the man who was pursuing her, and he was particularly anxious that this should not happen. He decided to hold his hand. He could not see what was taking place. He could only hear the swish and thud of racing feet, and the heavy breathing of somebody running desperately. Then came a little cry and the sound of a fall, followed by the exultant tones of the man panting triumphantly,

'Got you! Thought you'd get away, did you, you little fool!'

There was a silence then, and Quest

felt a pang of apprehension. Had he held his hand too long? Had something really serious happened to Celia Lamont in the depths of that gloomy wood? Something that he could have prevented if he had acted sooner? But the silence that had sounded so ominous was now broken by the sound of movement once again.

Footsteps were retreating, and Quest once more began to follow the noise.

The trees thinned into a small clearing; the footsteps stopped and a bright ray of dazzling light split up the darkness.

It came from a torch held in the hand of the man who had driven the coupé. It revealed Celia Lamont lying by the side of a long narrow trench that had been dug in the soft earth — a trench of such a shape that the sight of it sent Quest's heart leaping into his mouth. It was a grave, and it was there for the purpose of receiving the body of the girl who lay beside it! The detective's hand clenched round the butt of the automatic pistol, and he drew it from his pocket, thumbing back the safety catch. Watching, he saw the man with the torch transfer it to his left hand and take something from his breast pocket with his right that glittered evilly in the light — a long bladed knife!

Stooping, he raised the shining blade above the girl's body.

'Now!' he muttered, and at that precise second Quest fired!

17

The Man Who Wasn't There

The noise of the shot sounded like a bomb explosion in the silence of the wood and went echoing through the trees. It was followed by a scream of pain and the light went out. Still gripping the smoking pistol Quest plunged forward, making for the spot where he had last seen the man with the knife. But the man had fled, and the detective could hear him crashing through the undergrowth. From somewhere back in the wood came a shout and a ray of light flashed out and began to fan this way and that among the trees. It came to rest on Quest, and he heard Lester's voice cry out:

'There's Mr. Quest!'

The next moment he was by his side, almost immediately followed by David-son. The Inspector was breathless, but listened eagerly to Quest's account of what had happened.

'You've let him get away,' he said disappointedly.

'I'm afraid I did,' admitted the detective, with a tinge of chagrin in his voice. 'I delayed taking action until it was too late. At the last I had to do something quickly or that knife — '

He stopped and looked significantly to where Harding was kneeling beside the girl.

'You hit him,' said Lester. 'I heard him yell out.'

'Yes, in the wrist,' answered Quest. 'Look here.' He stooped beside the shallow grave and picked up the long-bladed knife that Merrick had dropped. The black hilt was red and wet.

'Luckily it was his blood,' said the Inspector, with a little shudder. 'What's the matter with Miss Lamont? Is she hurt?'

'I don't think so,' said Quest. 'I think she's only fainted from the shock.'

He went over and stooped beside Harding. The girl was deathly white and on her forehead was a large, ugly bruise, but she was breathing easily and regularly. The detective made a brief examination, and so far as he could see she was all right except for the lump on her forehead.

'Did they do that?' asked Harding venomously, and Quest shook his head.

'I don't think so,' he answered. 'I imagine she did that herself when she ran away.'

Celia Lamont stirred uneasily and opened her eyes. For a moment she looked round her dazedly, and then, with a cry of terror she sat up. Quest laid his hand on her shoulder.

'It's all right, Miss Lamont,' he said soothingly. 'You've nothing to be frightened about, you're with friends.'

She stared at him and from him to Harding, and the wild terror faded from her eyes.

'Jim,' she stammered huskily, 'how — how did you get here? Where's the man who — ?'

'It's all right, Celia,' said Harding echoing Quest's words. 'He's gone. We got here in time, thank Heaven!'

'Only just,' she murmured, and glanced

down at the newly-dug grave.

'Do you feel capable of walking a little way, Miss Lamont?' said Quest, partly to take her mind away from the recent horrible experience, and partly because he was anxious to be moving.

'Oh, yes,' she smiled rather wryly. 'I'm quite all right except for a headache.'

'Then I think we'll go back to the car and see what we can find at that house,' said the detective. 'You and I,' he turned to Davidson, 'can go in my car with Miss Lamont and Mr. Harding, and Lester can bring the coupé along.'

This was agreed upon, and Harding assisted the girl to her feet. She had to lean on him heavily, for the reaction had set in to her overstrained nerves, and she found that she was trembling violently.

However, it was only a short distance to the car — Lester had left it with its long radiator almost touching the coupé — and Celia sank into a corner of the back seat with a sigh of relief.

They had some difficulty in manœuvring the two cars out of that side turning — there was no room to turn them and they had to back all the way to the main road — but they succeeded.

As they ran back towards the lane leading to the house in which Celia had been kept a prisoner, the girl gave Quest a short account of what had happened to her from the time she had left Park Road to the time Quest had found her in the wood.

'Doctor Rule — eh?' said the detective when she had finished. 'H'm! I know all about him. He's a thorough-paced scoundrel, and has twice been in prison for running private mental asylums without a licence. At one time, I believe, he was a Harley Street specialist, and a remarkably clever man, but drink was his downfall, and he was several years ago struck off the medical register.'

'He's a horrible, beastly old man,' exclaimed the girl vehemently. 'But I wasn't so frightened of him as I was of the other.'

'You mean Merrick?' asked Harding, and she shook her head.

'No,' she replied, in a low tone. 'I mean the masked man with the high-pitched voice. I don't know why, but he terrified me.'

'That is the man I'm interested in,' said Quest. 'I should very much like to meet him. He appears to be the leading light in this business. Of course, you've no idea of his identity, Miss Lamont?'

'Why do you ask that?' she said in surprise.

'Because the obvious care he took to disguise his voice and keep his face concealed,' said Quest, 'suggests that in his normal capacity he was not unknown to you.'

'I think that's a bit far fetched, Mr. Quest,' disagreed Davidson. 'Don't you think it's equally likely that he was keeping his identity secret from these other fellows, Merrick and Rule? Probably he only hired them for the occasion, and being well up in the ways of crooks of that sort took the precaution to prevent them being able to blackmail him at a later date.'

'You may be right, Davidson,' agreed Quest. 'It's quite a likely supposition. All the same — ' He broke off. 'Here we are,' he said, and stopped the car at the mouth of the lane.

'Now,' he went on, turning round in his seat, 'what we've got to do is to take Rule and this other man by surprise, so I suggest that you and I and Lester make for this farm place while Harding stops behind and looks after Miss Lamont.'

This time Harding offered no objection to the scheme, a fact which brought a slight twinkle to the detective's eyes, though it couldn't be seen in the darkness.

'I think that's a very good idea,' asserted Davidson. 'But what about this fellow Merrick? Won't he have had time to get back to the farm and warn them?'

'He may have had time,' said Quest, 'but I don't think he'll go anywhere near the farm. He'll probably have jumped to the conclusion that we'd already visited the place and he'll keep as far away as possible. I know Merrick's type. He'll be too busy worrying about his own precious skin to think about his companions.'

He opened the door and stepped out on to the streaming roadway. Lester had brought the coupé to a halt a yard behind the other car, and at a sign from Quest got out and joined him. By this time Davidson had extricated himself from the back seat and was turning up his coat against the cutting wind.

After a hasty word with Lester, Quest led the way towards the mouth of the lane, and once more they plunged into the encompassing darkness.

The light was still shining out — a yellow patch in the night — and Quest felt rather relieved when he saw it. It tended to confirm his supposition that nothing had occurred to alarm the inmates of the house.

They proceeded cautiously and in silence until they reached the gate giving access to the littered back yard. From here they had a good view of the straggling bulk of the house. The back door was shut and no lights were visible, because from this point the window with the yellow glow could not be seen.

Quest opened the gate cautiously, and the trio began to pick their way among the refuse that littered the ground.

'Pretty dismal looking place, isn't it?' whispered Davidson, and the detective nodded.

They reached the back door, and Quest tried the handle. It turned under his hand, and at a slight push the door opened inwards. It had been left unlocked! The reason for this flashed to the detective's mind instantly. It had been left for the return of Merrick from his murderous excursion. It was a great piece of luck, for it would enable them to get inside the cottage without warning the inmates of their presence.

Quest stepped across the threshold into the dark hallway beyond, with Lester and Davidson close on his heels. Carefully he closed the door behind him and then stood for a moment motionless, listening. From somewhere inside came the murmur of voices. They sounded muffled and they could not hear what was being said but from the tones he judged them to be those of a man and a woman. The woman was, of course, the Mrs. Crow whom Celia had mentioned.

Quest began to move stealthily along

the passage, feeling his way by the wall. He came to a short flight of steps, and whispered a warning to the others close behind him. Mounting the steps — there were only four of them — he found that the narrow passage widened suddenly into a square hall. On his left was a door from under which came a narrow line of light. The voices, too, came from behind this door, and were now plainer and more distinct.

The woman was arguing vehemently, and even as Quest approached the closed door she raised her voice shrilly.

'That's all very well,' she said angrily; 'but I ain't going to stay up all the blessed night. I want my rest the same as anybody else, and I'm going ter get it — see!'

'You'll do as you're told, that's what you'll do,' came the answer in thick, slightly blurred tones. 'I've got to stay up, haven't I, and if I've got to stay up you can stay up too!'

From the thickness of the tone, which was obviously that of a man who had been drinking more than was good for him, Quest concluded that the owner of the voice was Doctor Rule.

'Anyway,' the voice went on, 'Merrick can't be long now. He ought to have been back long ago.'

'Where did he go?' demanded the woman. 'Where was he taking that girl?'

'Mind your own business,' snarled the doctor. 'It's no concern of yours!'

'Oh, isn't it?' cried Mrs. Crow. 'I'm not sure of that. I've helped you over a lot of things, but I don't like this business at all. Who's the feller with the handkerchief over his eyes? Coming 'ere and giving orders to people as if they was dirt.'

'Will you hold your infernal tongue!' roared Rule. 'Who he is has got nothing to do with you. Whatever you've done in this matter you've got well paid for, so shut up!'

There came the clink of glass against glass and the splash of liquid.

''Ow much more of that stuff are yer going ter drink?' said the woman. 'You've got through nearly a whole bottle this evening.'

'I'll get through two if I want to,' snapped the doctor. 'Get out, and come back when I call you.'

'You can call as long as you like,' retorted Mrs. Crow, 'but I'm not going ter do nothing more tonight. I'm going to bed and if you don't like it you can lump it!'

The doctor mumbled something in reply, and then the door was jerked open, and a stream of light lit up the hall. It fell full on Philip Quest, and the woman, who was in the act of stepping out, saw him. She uttered a little shrill cry of fear and stopped dead.

'What the Hades is the matter with you now?' snarled Rule, turning, glass in hand, from the side table over which he had been bending. And then he, too, saw the detective, and a startled oath left his lips. His jaw dropped, and the glass, half full of yellow liquid, slipped from his hand and shattered to fragments on the floor.

'Philip Quest!' he gasped.

The detective stepped forward, thrusting the scared woman aside.

'I see you remember me,' he said pleasantly. 'I want you, Rule. There'll be several charges, I've no doubt, but the main one at the moment is accessory to the murder of Richard Lamont!'

The doctor licked his thick lips, which had suddenly assumed a blue tinge.

'I don't know what you're talking about,' he muttered thickly, and swayed slightly. 'I don't know anything about murder — '

'Then perhaps your friend does,' snapped Quest. 'The man who so carefully conceals his identity behind a mask. Where is he?'

'There's nobody else here,' said Rule huskily. 'Nobody at all, except myself and my housekeeper.'

'Whether he's here now or not makes no difference,' retorted the detective. 'He was here a little while ago.'

'I assure you — ' began the doctor, but Quest cut him short.

'Bluff isn't going to help you,' he rapped quickly. 'We've heard the whole story from Miss Lamont. Come on now, you know who that masked man is, and where he is to be found, and you're going to tell us.'

'I — ' The bald-headed man's face twisted into a spasm of pain. A hoarse inarticulate cry left his throat, and, with one hand tearing at the collar of his dressing gown, he suddenly pitched forward on his face and lay a sprawling heap in front of the fireplace.

Instantly Quest was at his side and stooping over the still, shapeless figure. With deft fingers he loosened the man's shirt and felt for his heart. A second later he looked up gravely.

'We shan't get any information out of Rule,' he said. 'Whisky and the shock have been too much for him. He's dead!'

18

Philip Quest Reviews The Case

The big shaded lamp on Philip Quest's desk shed a soft light over the littered blotting pad. It was the only light in the consulting-room, save the fire, and it caught and outlined the detective's lean, eager face as he sat in his padded chair.

It was late in the evening of the day following upon the incidents at the farm house at Southwater, and many things had happened since Doctor Rule had succumbed to a diseased heart in the sitting room of the cottage. Mrs. Crow, protesting shrilly and indignantly, had been placed under arrest, and the cottage diligently and thoroughly searched. Enough evidence had been found there of Rule's misdemeanours to convict him several times over, but nothing that linked him with the Lamont business or gave any clue regarding the identity of the masked man — that mysterious and elusive individual whom Quest was so anxious to trace. Neither had anything more been seen or heard of Merrick. He had not attempted to return to Tate Street — not that Quest ever dreamed that he would — and the constable who had been put on duty to watch the Wilkins' house had his vigil for nothing.

The inquest on Richard Lamont had taken place that morning, but it was purely a formal affair, and had not taken very long.

Dr. Harman had given his evidence regarding the discovery of the body and the cause of death, and this latter had been confirmed by the Divisional surgeon. The body had been formally identified, and the police had asked for and been granted a fortnight's adjournment pending further evidence.

Philip Quest himself had not been present, but had occupied his morning in Fleet Street, examining the file of the paper that the elder Lamont had been reading on the morning he had, according to Celia, received such a shock. He had found what he believed to have been the paragraph that had so disturbed Lamont — a brief statement to the effect that Leslie Cowley, the convict who had escaped from the Breakwater at Cape Town, was still at large and was believed to have succeeded in escaping to England. Quest had managed to get hold of a copy of a paper, and had brought it back with him to his office.

Throughout the dreary November afternoon he had sat hunched up by the fire, his mind completely centred on the problem.

Lester had towards tea-time taken himself off to the pictures, and the tea which had been brought to Quest had been taken away again, cold and untouched, much to the maid's disgust.

The result of Quest's mental orgy was now visible on the desk before him in the form of several closely written pages in which he had set out the facts in his possession and the conclusions he derived from them. The result was certainly not very illuminating, although he had the basis for several new theories. He had, at least, now got the reason for Francis Lamont's change of personality when he came back to England that last time. Harding's story had cleared that up, and the newspaper paragraph that he had found that morning had shown the cause of Lamont's sudden ejaculation and appearance of having received a shock in that last morning before his death. But there were gaps — big gaps.

Why had he been so scared at the thought that Cowley was in England? He had done nothing to Bishop or Cowley that he should fear them. Cowley had stated that they had been caught quite accidentally, and by no action of Lamont's, and this was borne out by the fact that they had not given him away as their accomplice at the trial.

Quest could guess why they had not done this. Their sentence was only one of two years, and after they were free there was their share of the stolen diamonds to come back to. If they had given Lamont away he would have been arrested as well, and the diamonds probably found and confiscated.

Therefore they had kept quiet. The detective was pretty sure that this was the reason, and not by any sense of fair play or loyalty. He had had too much to do with crooks of all classes to labour under the delusion that there was any such thing as honour among thieves. Most criminals would sell their own brothers for a profit. So why had Lamont been so afraid that the very thought of Cowley being in England was sufficient to drive him to taking his own life?

There was only one answer, and that was that Lamont had betrayed his trust in some way. He had failed to live up to the legend that there is honour among thieves and had double-crossed his companions.

Unconsciously Quest nodded to himself as he stared at the desk. Yes, that was it, and the question was: what had Lamont done? If he had merely brought them out of the country and carted them off to England when he left there was no reason to fear Cowley. He had only to hand the man his share of the booty, and everything would be all right. Why, then, his panic — such a panic that the only way out he saw was death? Had he disposed of the diamonds and spent the money, or lost them? That could not be the solution, otherwise, what was this unknown man after. It was undoubtedly a puzzle, and, rack his brains as he would, Quest could not hit on a likely solution.

There were the veils, too. How did they come into it? Apparently they were of the utmost importance, since to get hold of them had been the reason for abducting Celia Lamont.

Quest glanced across at the safe that occupied a corner of the consulting-room, and half rose. But, changing his mind, sank back in his chair again. What was the good of examining those flimsy pieces of silk any more thoroughly than he had done already.

He had spent hours over them without any result. Their secret would remain a secret until the people behind this strange affair were caught and under lock and key.

His mind switched back to the elusive man in the mask of whom Celia had been in such fear. Mrs. Crow had been closely questioned regarding this mysterious personage, but she definitely stated that she knew nothing whatever about him except that he visited Dr. Rule on several occasions. She had never seen his face; he had always worn the concealing handkerchief, and he had always talked in the same high-pitched voice that Celia had described. She thought that the doctor had known who he was because they appeared to be old friends. It had been the doctor who had first introduced him to Merrick. No amount of questioning and cross-questioning could shake this statement, and Quest believed that the woman was speaking the truth. She was one of those people who simply hadn't the intelligence to keep up sustained lying once they were caught. Quest himself had little doubt as to the identity of the shadow man, as Celia called him. He must be Cowley. That was obvious. But this certainly did not help matters. Nobody had any idea what Cowley was like. The only man who did know was dead, Souza, and it was probably for this reason he had been killed.

It was true that Quest had that

morning cabled to Cape Town for a
photograph of Cowley, but he was not
counting that it would be of much use. It
wasn't difficult to make slight changes in
one's appearance. A different way of
brushing the hair; a portion shaved off the
eyebrows; a moustache — and the
alteration was marvellous. No, the detective rose wearily to his feet and lit a
cigarette, the case had reached a dead-
lock. There were only two chances at the
moment — either that Merrick and the
unknown Cowley would be caught, and
both seemed to Quest so slender as
scarcely to be chances at all.

He dropped into his chair again and
stretched out his feet to the fire with a long
sigh. He was still sitting there when Lester
came back from his picture excursion.

'Hello!' he said. 'Have you made any
progress?'

Quest shook his head.

'No,' he replied irritably. 'I must
confess that for the moment I'm beaten.
How did you enjoy the *Secret Man?*'

Lester made a grimace.

'Not much,' he said. 'It was the usual

bunk. I guessed who the secret man was half way through. There was one good bit though — the trap they set for the murderer in order to find out who he is.'

Quest smiled.

'What did they do?' he asked.

'The detective spreads it around that he's got a clue locked up in his safe that will tell him the identity of the Secret Man — a charm — the Secret Man hears about this, and tries to break open the safe, and they nab him. Of course, there was no clue there at all. He did exactly what the detective was counting he would, and gave himself away — ' He stopped, for Philip Quest had suddenly sat bolt upright, his lean face flushed and a sparkle in his eyes.

'By Jove, that's it!' he exclaimed.

Lester surveyed him in astonishment.

'What's it?' he demanded.

'You've given me an idea, that's all,' explained the detective more calmly. 'Really it seems that the 'talkies' have their uses after all!'

19

Quest Baits a Trap

Philip Quest rose early on the morning following Lester's return from the pictures full of the idea which his partner's casual remarks had suggested.

There were a certain number of difficulties to be got over before it could be put into practice, but Quest thought that with a little care these could be overcome.

He had breakfasted and gone out long before Lester had got up, and that young man was just sitting down to a large plate of kidneys and bacon when he returned.

'Hello, partner, you've been out early!' greeted Lester.

'It's just as well that one of the firm should be up and doing,' retorted Quest, with a twinkle in his eye as he discarded his overcoat.

'I'm very glad to hear that there is

something doing,' said Lester, 'what's in the wind?'

'A touch of frost, I should say,' replied Quest gravely, lighting a cigarette. 'How long are you going to be over your breakfast?'

'Not long,' said Lester looking up. 'Why, have you got something for me to do?'

Quest nodded.

'Yes,' he said. 'I want you to get out the car and go over to Sydenham. See Inspector Davidson and bring him back here with you.'

'All right,' said Lester gulping a large piece of kidney. 'What am I to tell him?'

'I'll give you a note,' said Quest, and going over to his desk took a sheet of paper from the stationery rack. Hastily he scribbled a few lines, signed his name, folded the paper and put it in an envelope, licking down the flap.

'Here you are,' he said and laid the letter beside the young man's plate.

Lester looked at it curiously and from it to Quest.

There was an air of quiet excitement about the detective that warned him that Quest was feeling intensely pleased about something. He refrained, however, from asking questions. Long association with Quest's characteristics had made him aware that on these occasions the detective was very oyster-like. He loved to keep his plans to himself until they had reached fruition. So he refrained from putting the questions that were hovering on his lips, and went on eating his breakfast. He finished it well within the time he had stated, and struggling into his overcoat, picked up his hat and the note and made his way round to the garage.

When Lester had gone and he was alone Quest rang for the maid, in a few seconds she was at the door.

'Come in,' said Quest, 'and shut the door. I want a word with you.'

The girl obeyed his instructions and stood waiting expectantly.

'What I want to tell you is this,' went on the detective. 'Mr. Lester and I will be going away this afternoon, and I want you to tell my callers that we shall be away for several days. Do you understand?'

'Yes, sir.'

'But,' explained the detective, 'I am not

really going away at all. That is only what I want you to tell people. We shall leave this afternoon with our luggage, but we shall not go further than the station. Our luggage will be put in the train, but we shall come back during the evening and come in by the back entrance.'

'Where shall I say you've gone?' asked the maid.

'To Scotland,' replied Quest.

It was nearly half past twelve when Lester came back with Davidson. Both he and the stout Inspector looked slightly puzzled, and Blake guessed why when he saw the noon edition of the evening paper clutched in Davidson's hand.

'What's all this about, Mr. Quest?' demanded the Inspector. 'Is this true?' He pointed to a paragraph on the front page of the racing edition.

'Partly,' said the detective, glancing at it. The paragraph read:

'Philip Quest Indisposed.
'Mr. Philip Quest, the famous private detective, is, we understand, suffering from the effects of nervous strain due

237

to overwork. His doctor has insisted that he shall give up all his professional duties for the time being, and he is, therefore, leaving this afternoon for Scotland, accompanied by his partner, Richard Lester. Mr. Quest's intention is to put all work aside and take a complete rest. He has been helping the police in the Sydenham Murders, and he told our representative this morning that he had what he considers an important clue which he intends to follow up immediately on his return from his holiday.'

'You never told me anything about this!' exclaimed Lester.

Quest smiled.

'I never knew anything about it myself until last night,' he said.

'Then how did it get into the paper?' demanded Davidson.

'It got into the paper,' replied Quest, 'because I persuaded them to put it in first thing this morning.'

The stout Inspector scratched his head.

'But is it true?' he said. 'Are you going

to Scotland this afternoon?'

'I am not,' said Philip Quest. 'I am going as far as the station, but that's all.'

Davidson stared at him in bewilderment.

'I don't understand it,' he said. 'What's the idea?'

'The idea is quite simple, and was suggested to me by something Lester said last night,' explained Quest. 'I am very anxious to make the acquaintance of the unknown man with the squeaky voice who was responsible for the abduction of Celia Lamont, and who is undoubtedly behind these two murders.'

'But how is this going to help you to do that?' cried Davidson, stabbing at the paper with a fat forefinger.

'In this way,' said Quest. 'We know he is very anxious to secure those two veils that Francis Lamont gave his daughter — that was the reason he went to all that trouble to get her to that farm — he knows that they are in my possession. Celia Lamont told him that she had given them to me herself. I therefore propose to give him as clear a field as possible so that

239

he can come and get them.'

An expression of comprehension flashed across the Inspector's face.

'I see,' he said, and then, frowning doubtfully: 'But do you think it will work? Do you think he'll come?'

'I think he'll either come himself or send somebody else,' answered the detective. 'Of course, I can't be absolutely certain, but anyhow, there's no harm done, and it's worth trying.'

'I suppose the idea is that you will come back here without being seen and lie in wait for him,' said Davidson.

'Exactly,' agreed Quest. 'We shall depart for the station this afternoon, complete with luggage. We shall make our departure as ostentatious as possible. Our luggage will be put on the train but we ourselves will remain behind. We shall fill in the rest of the afternoon and evening at the station hotel, and under cover of darkness and by the back entrance we'll come back here and wait developments — if any.' He paused and then went on, 'The reason I sent for you, Davidson, was to arrange where we shall pick you up.'

240

'You want me to be present?' asked the Inspector.

'I think it would be advisable,' said Quest. 'You are officially in charge of the case. I am merely helping you from a friendly point of view. I have no standing at all in the matter. I haven't been engaged by anybody to look into the matter. Yes, I think it would be a good idea if you were here.'

He did not add that his real reason was that if there was any credit going for the capture of the unknown man Davidson should have it all, but the Inspector, who knew Quest of old, must have guessed, for he said:

'It's jolly nice of you to put it that way.'

'I think the best thing for you to do will be to pick us up at the hotel,' said the detective. 'Get there about nine, that will be early enough.'

'I'll be there,' said Davidson heartily, 'and I hope your plan's successful and something comes of it.'

'I hope so, too,' said Quest.

They spent another half-hour discussing the details, and then the Inspector took his departure.

At three o'clock precisely a taxi drew up outside Quest's flat, and a large trunk and several suitcases were brought out and solemnly put on the cab.

Quest gave the smiling maid a few last instructions in a particularly loud voice, and then he and Lester got into the taxicab and it drove away.

A well-dressed man who had been sauntering along on the other side of the road saw it go and continued his walk with a smile of satisfaction.

20

The Vigil

Philip Quest finished his coffee, lighted a cigar and looked across the table in the corner of the big dining room at the Station Hotel at Lester.

'Davidson should be here in half an hour,' he remarked.

The young man stifled a yawn.

'Thank goodness for that!' he grunted.

Quest smiled.

'That is not very complimentary to my powers as a host,' he said reproachfully.

'Aren't you getting a bit bored yourself?' asked Lester.

'Well, I dislike inaction at any time,' confessed the detective, 'and I hate station hotels, so I must admit that I am.'

Lester opened his mouth to reply, but refrained as a waiter came towards them.

'There's a gentleman in the lounge enquiring for you, sir,' he said.

'That will be Davidson,' remarked the detective to Lester. 'He's early. All right, waiter, we'll join him immediately. Bring the bill, will you?'

When Quest had settled the bill and tipped the waiter they made their way to the lounge.

Davidson, looking fatter than ever in a thick blue overcoat, came hurrying towards them.

'I came earlier, Mr. Quest,' he greeted, 'because I've got some rather startling news for you.'

'Oh, what's that?' asked Quest quickly.

'Merrick was found at four o'clock this afternoon shot dead in a little wood on the outskirts of Sydenham,' replied Davidson.

Lester uttered an exclamation, but Quest, beyond a sudden gleam in his eyes, appeared quite unmoved by the Inspector's news. Looking hastily round the almost empty lounge, he drew them over to a group of chairs by the fireplace and sat down.

'Now, then,' he said, motioning the other two to sit beside him, 'I'll order you a drink, Davidson, and you can tell me all about it. What will you have?'

The Inspector suggested that whisky-and-soda would go down very well, and Quest, calling the attendant, ordered a double Scotch.

'We can talk here without being overheard,' he said when the drink had been brought, 'and we needn't leave for another hour.'

'Well, there isn't much to tell,' said Davidson, sipping appreciatively at the contents of his glass. 'The body was found by some boys who had gone into the wood to play. They informed a constable and he notified the police station. I was in at the time and I went along.'

'How do you know it's Merrick?' asked Quest.

'I got that fellow Wilkins to identify him,' replied the Inspector. 'You see, I guessed who it was directly I set eyes on the body. It answered to Merrick's description, and when the divisional surgeon said he'd got a wound in the right hand that looked as if it had been caused by a bullet I was pretty certain.

Wilkins confirmed my suspicions at once.'

'I wonder what he was doing at Sydenham,' said Lester.

'That's what I wondered,' said the Inspector. 'It's a pretty good way from Southwater.'

'I should think,' said Quest, 'that he came to Sydenham to see his accomplice — the unknown man with the squeaky voice.'

'And he shot him, eh?' Davidson gulped the remainder of the whisky and nodded. 'Yes, I shouldn't be surprised if you were right, though I don't see what his motive was.'

'Probably Merrick knew too much,' said the detective, 'and threatened him. What time was he killed?'

'The doctor couldn't say with certainty,' replied Davidson, 'but it was several hours before he was found. Most likely during the morning.'

'H'm!' Quest tossed his half-smoked cigar into the fire. 'Well, we are certain of one thing, anyway, whoever falls into the trap it won't be Merrick.'

'Perhaps nobody will fall into it,'

suggested Lester.

'It's quite probable,' said Quest. 'And certainly we are optimistic in supposing that they will fall into it tonight. But there's a chance. We know that this man is very anxious to gain possession of those veils, and he may not believe in wasting time.'

'Have you any idea who he is?' said Davidson, struck by something in Quest's tone.

'Yes,' he answered, 'I have an idea that he was Cowley. What he calls himself now though, I must admit I haven't the vaguest notion.'

'Cowley, eh?' said Lester. 'That's the fellow who escaped from the Breakwater at Cape Town.'

'Yes,' said Quest. 'The other man died, if you remember.'

'And you think the man who is at the bottom of this business is Cowley?' said Davidson thoughtfully.

'I don't see how it can be anyone else,' said the detective.

'Then he killed Richard Lamont!' said Lester.

'Ah, now you're going too fast.' Philip Quest shook his head. 'We come up against many difficulties there.'

'How do you mean?' asked Davidson.

'Well, we don't know what happened to Souza,' explained Quest. 'It was Souza who called for Richard Lamont — we have the maid's word for that — and it was presumably Souza who took him to the empty house in Elm Tree Avenue. If this man Cowley killed Lamont, then he must have been in the house when they arrived. And Souza must have seen him commit the crime.'

'Unless Lamont went into the house first, leaving Souza outside with the car,' said Lester.

'Even in that case,' answered Quest, 'you are up against a very extraordinary fact. Even supposing that Souza did not actually see the murder committed he must have been aware of it before anyone else. Why didn't he inform the police?'

'Perhaps he was on his way to do so when he was killed himself,' said Davidson.

'So long after?' Quest raised his

248

eyebrows. 'Why the delay? Why didn't he go at once? Besides, I don't think he was going to the police when he was killed. I think he was going to find Harding.'

'What makes you think that?' put in Lester.

'The card in his hand,' said Quest. 'It was Harding's card. Now, why was it found in his hand. A man does not as a rule carry another man's card in his hand. He puts it in his pocket until he wants to refer to it. Now, I noticed that there was a street lamp just before the place where Souza was killed, and my explanation is that he stopped under it, took out the card to confirm Harding's address, and as he was moving on again was overtaken by his murderer and killed. Hence the card being found in his hand.'

'That's a very reasonable explanation, Mr. Quest,' agreed Inspector Davidson. 'But it doesn't help to explain what happened in that empty house during the time Richard Lamont met his death.'

'No, it doesn't,' said Quest. 'We shan't know that until we catch Cowley.' He looked at his watch and rose to his feet.

'It's time we were going,' he said. 'It would never do for the mouse to nibble at the cheese and find no trap to close down on him.'

He retrieved his and Lester's coat from the cloakroom, and the porter sent for a taxi. They got in, and Quest told the driver to set them down at Holborn.

'We shall have to walk from there,' he said, 'but it isn't very far.'

When they had reached their destination and the detective had paid the cabman, he led the way into a maze of back streets and presently dived into a dark opening of a mews. The place was nearly deserted, for most of the garages of which it was composed were locked up, the cars they housed either being inside or still out.

'Here we are,' said Quest when they had traversed this for a few yards, and taking a key from his pocket inserted it in the lock of a green-painted door that was set in the high brick wall. Quest had often used this way before. Few people looking at the offices from the front imagined for an instant that there was this back exit, and for this reason it had proved invaluable to Quest on those occasions when he had wished to either leave or come without being seen.

The back door was unlocked, and as they entered the maid appeared smilingly to greet them.

'Several callers have been, Mr. Quest,' she said. 'But I told all of them that you were away for a holiday, and I didn't know when you would be returning.'

'That's right,' said Quest. 'You haven't put any lights on in any of the rooms, have you?'

'No, sir, the whole place is in darkness.'

Lester smiled.

'We'll go through to the consulting-room,' said Quest. 'I'm afraid we shall have to find our way without a light and sit in the dark, but that can't be helped.'

He led the way into the hall and up the staircase. Opening the door of the consulting-room he ushered the others inside and carefully closed it.

'Now,' he said, guiding the bulky form of Davidson over to a chair, 'make yourself as comfortable as you can. Lester and I will sit on the settee. I don't think we'd better smoke, and as we daren't risk a fire we'd better keep our coats on.'

The chair creaked as the Inspector sank into its depths with a grunt.

From outside came the roar and bustle of the traffic, but inside the room it was as quiet as the grave. The clock on the mantelpiece ticked away the seconds with a steady beat. Philip Quest settled himself in one corner of the settee, and Lester curled himself up in the other.

By tacit consent none of them spoke. The time dragged by drearily. After what seemed an eternity the clock below in the hall chimed twelve with a sonorous deliberation, and Davidson's chair creaked as the Inspector shifted uneasily.

Was their vigil going to prove futile for that night? Quest admitted to himself that he wouldn't be surprised if it did. It was asking rather too much to expect results so soon, and yet something told him that the man they were expecting was not the kind to waste time.

Half-past twelve — one.

The noise of the traffic had faded to an

occasional hoot of a belated taxi.

Two!

From the direction of Inspector Davidson's chair came the faint rumble of a snore. Quest leaned forward sharply, and, reaching out, grabbed an arm. The snore ended in a gasp.

'For Heaven's sake don't go to sleep!' whispered the detective sharply. 'If you start snoring you'll scare our friend away.'

He was answered by a grunt, but the threatened nocturne was not continued.

Half-past two!

And nothing, not a sound, came from the silent house, save the ticking of the clock on the mantelpiece, and the deep chiming of the hall clock. The trap was baited but nobody was going to rise to the bait. Their vigil was a wasted one after all.

Quest began to wonder how many nights would have to be spent like this, and if, after all, the man he was after would come at all.

Perhaps he would not take the risk. Perhaps as yet he had not seen a paper with the paragraph of Quest's and Lester's departure. Perhaps he would never see it, and remain in ignorance of the fact that he had a clear field. Perhaps —

Quest suddenly sat up, alert and vigilant, every nerve in his body tense. The hall clock had just struck three, and as the sound of the bell died to silence there came another sound — a faint, almost inaudible creak! It came from the staircase. Instantly Quest was off the settee and bending over Davidson.

'Quick!' he whispered, his lips close to the Inspector's ear. 'Over in the corner by the door, and move swiftly. He's coming!'

21

A Smart Capture

The three watchers crouched silently in the dark corner behind the door. There was no sound now from the still house. After that first faint creak there was no other sign of the presence of the intruder. A long minute went by and Quest had almost begun to persuade himself that he had been mistaken when there came the soft pad of feet from the corridor outside. They were barely audible and would have passed unnoticed but for the fact that his hearing was keyed up to an abnormal pitch.

At the door they stopped. There was a long pause, and Quest could hear the sound of irregular breathing the breathing of a man who was consumed with an inward excitement. The handle rattled slightly and then the door began to slowly open. Inch by inch it swung wider and a dark muffled figure slipped into the room. Quest felt the bulky form of Inspector Davidson stiffen beside him, and he laid a warning hand on the other's arm. The time was not yet ripe to make their presence known. The intruder stopped by the door, and from his rigid attitude Quest guessed that he was listening intently. After a moment he moved and gently closed the door. There was another pause, and then a little click that leapt across the darkness and quivered — a round white circle on the opposite wall.

Quest almost held his breath. If the man who had entered had looked round he could not fail to see them. The reflected light from that quivering patch would show them up clearly, but the man did not look round. He moved his light along and down until it rested upon the door of the safe. From his lips came a sudden soft hiss as his pent up breath was released. He had found what he was seeking.

With scarcely more sound than would have been made by a cat he advanced, and kneeling down, began to examine the lock. The watchers saw now that his hands were gloved and that his face was invisible beneath the folds of a silk scarf. He laid the torch on the floor so that its light still remained directed on the safe's door, and, feeling in his pocket, produced a leather roll. As he unrolled it there came the gentle tinkle of metal.

Philip Quest's hand strayed to his hip pocket and emerged, gripping the butt of an automatic. Now was the time, while the other was still kneeling there — selecting the tools with which he was going to make his attack on the safe. Stealthily the detective began to creep across the intervening space of carpet towards the bent back silhouetted against the light of the torch. Step by step and inch by inch he drew nearer, while Davidson and Lester watched with tensed muscles.

The man by the safe, completely unconscious of that approaching figure, had selected a drill and was fitting it to a brace. Barely two yards separated them now. Noiselessly Quest straightened up from his crouching position, and covered the remaining distance in two swift strides. His hand dropped heavily on the other's shoulder, and the cold circle of the pistol's barrel was rammed into the nape of his neck.

'I want you, Cowley!' he said sharply.

The kneeling man ripped out a startled oath, and tried to spring to his feet.

'I wouldn't struggle, if I were you,' warned Quest, and accentuated his words by pressing the pistol further into the man's neck. 'Lester, put on the lights!'

A hand went to the switches beside the door and the centre pendant blazed to life.

Still keeping a firm grip on the man's shoulder Quest jerked him to his feet.

'Come and take off this scarf and let's see what we've got, Davidson,' snapped the detective, and the Inspector advanced.

A swift jerk, and the obscuring scarf was pulled away from the mouth, nose and chin.

'Now,' said Davidson, 'who the dickens are you?'

The sallow, hate-distorted face of the man he had unmasked glared defiantly at him in silence.

Mr. James Harding stirred uneasily in his sleep. He had been dreaming quite pleasantly, and now had come this uncouth noise to shatter the sylvan which his subconscious mind had created. He grunted and turned over on his back.

Bang, bang, bang!

He opened his eyes dazedly and stared at the ceiling of his bedroom. What the devil was the matter?

Rat-tat-tat-tat — bang, bang!

Dimly it penetrated to his still sleep-confused mind that the noise was the result of someone banging on the front door knocker. Muttering several uncomplimentary things concerning the disturber of his peace Mr. Harding hoisted himself on to one elbow and looked at the small clock on the table at his bedside. It was barely eight o'clock.

Again the peremptory summons echoed through the flat, and with a groan he rose, pulled on a dressing gown, inserted his feet into slippers and made his way to the tiny hall.

'Who the deuce — ' he began angrily, and then stopped.

Philip Quest stood on the threshold.

'I'm sorry if I woke you up, Harding,' said the detective hastily. 'But I want you to come along with me to the police station. Can you slip on some clothes? I've got the car outside.'

Harding frowned.

'What's the idea?' he asked suspiciously. 'Am I going to be arrested again, or something?'

Quest laughed.

'No, not this time,' he said. 'If you'll let me come in I'll explain.'

Harding stood aside, and when he had entered closed the door.

'You'd better come into the sitting room,' he said, and led the way to the room in which Quest had first interviewed him. 'Now,' he continued, 'what's all the excitement?'

'The excitement is that we've got the man who was responsible for the death of Richard Lamont and the abduction of Miss Lamont,' said Quest smoothly. 'And I want you to come along and have a look at him.'

'You've got him?' cried Harding excitedly.

Quest nodded.

'Yes, we've got him,' he said. 'Without any shadow of doubt.'

'By Jove, that's good work!' exclaimed Harding. 'How did you manage it?'

'He just walked into our hands,' said Quest. 'I'll tell you all that presently. At the moment I am rather in a hurry, so if you will — '

'Won't keep you two minutes,' said Harding and crossed to the door. With his hand on the handle he paused and looked back. 'Why do you want me to see him?' he asked curiously.

'Just to test an idea of mine,' said the detective. 'I want to see if you recognise him.'

Harding's face expressed the astonishment the words caused him.

'I recognise him!' he echoed. 'How should I recognise him? I've never seen him before in my life.'

'I rather think you have,' said Quest with the ghost of a twinkle in his eyes.

261

'But — ' began the other vehemently.

'Suppose you slip some clothes on and come and see,' broke in the detective suggestively, and, taking the hint, Harding left the room without another word.

He was back again almost at once, dressed in a lounge suit and feeling his chin gingerly.

'I haven't waited to shave,' he said. 'You've made me so curious that I couldn't waste the time.'

'You'll be able to shave when you get back,' said Quest, rising to his feet. 'I shan't keep you long.'

They left the flat together, and Harding got into the waiting car beside Quest. The journey to the station was not a long one, but to the impatient Harding it seemed miles. He was intensely anxious to find out why Quest should think that he would be able to recognise this unknown man — the murderer of Richard Lamont and the abductor of Celia.

He was out of the car almost before it came to a halt.

'This way,' said Quest, and led him

through the charge room to the Inspector's little office.

The stout Inspector was sitting at his desk as they entered, but he got up at once.

'Ah, so you've brought him, Mr. Quest,' he said with a chuckle. 'Now we shall be able to see if your theory is right or wrong.'

He lifted a bunch of keys from a numbered hook on a green baize board.

'Come on,' he said. 'The last time you came this way it was not so pleasant, eh, Mr. Harding?'

They went down the stone steps and along the corridor to the cells. Outside one of them — the same one Harding had occupied — Davidson stopped, inserted one of the keys and swung the heavy door open.

Inside on the plank bed a man was seated. Harding could only see the top of his head for his chin was sunk on his breast, and he was staring at the floor.

'We've brought a visitor to see you,' said Quest, and at his voice the man looked up.

Harding uttered a startled exclamation and his face went white.

'Great Heavens,' he breathed. 'It's impossible! Utterly impossible!'

'So you do recognise this man, eh?' said Quest, his eyes gleaming.

'Certainly I do,' muttered Harding. 'He is Manuel Souza!'

22

The Man Who Died

'I thought you'd say that,' remarked Philip Quest. 'You are absolutely sure?'

'Absolutely,' declared Harding, his face the picture of amazement and bewilderment. 'That is the man I saw in Johannesburg and who called and borrowed my car. But I don't understand it. I thought you said Souza was murdered?'

'We thought he was,' put in Davidson. 'His pockets contained an envelope addressed to Souza.'

'There was a certain resemblance, too,' said Quest, looking at the mute, savage-faced man who was glaring up at them. 'If it hadn't been for the excitement caused by the abduction of Miss Lamont you would have been asked to identify the body before, and we should have been in possession of this information several days ago.'

'But if this man is Souza,' frowned Harding, 'who was the man who was killed?'

'I don't think it's very difficult to guess that,' said Quest. 'The man who was killed was Leslie Cowley. Isn't that right?' he added sharply, turning to the sallow-faced occupant of the plank bed.

'Find out,' was the snarling reply. 'You seem to know so much you'd better find out the rest.'

'That's enough of that!' rapped Davidson. 'You keep a civil tongue in your head.'

'I shall say what I like,' retorted Souza. 'There's no law that can prevent me talking.'

'I'm still rather puzzled,' said Harding. 'I thought that Doris, Celia's maid, had identified the dead man as the man who called for Dick Lamont that night in my car.'

'So she did,' agreed Quest.

'It was Souza who got the address and borrowed my car,' protested the other. 'How in the world — '

'Souza came to you for Lamont's

address because you'd met him before,' said Quest. 'You wouldn't have been so eager to give it to a stranger. As soon as he'd got it and got the loan of your car he handed it over to his friend Cowley — '

'Very good indeed,' broke in the sallow-faced man with a sneer. 'You might almost have been there.'

'Then Cowley and Souza were working together?' exclaimed Harding.

'That's how I explain it,' replied Quest.

'But why did Souza kill him?' asked the young man.

Quest shrugged his shoulders.

'Ask Souza,' he said. 'I can't tell you that. I can guess, but I'm not certain.'

'You can ask till you're black in the face,' snarled Souza. 'But you'll hear nothing from me. I don't admit that I did kill him and you're going to find it very difficult to prove that I did.'

'But not so difficult to prove that you killed Richard Lamont,' snapped Quest quickly.

Souza raised his eyebrows.

'Really,' he said. 'You surprise me. How do you intend to prove that?'

'Because you are wearing the same shoes now that you did that night,' retorted the detective, 'and the police have tracings and photographs of the prints found in that empty house. A comparison will show, I think, that they are the same in every detail. That will be sufficient to convince any jury.'

The murderer's yellow face went a dirty grey, and he flinched.

'You forgot that, didn't you?' Quest went on. 'One of the few things you did forget.'

'Yes, you're quite right, I forgot that,' muttered Souza hoarsely. 'I suppose I might as well make a clean breast of it. I killed Richard Lamont and Cowley; I also killed Merrick — '

'You're not bound to say anything that will incriminate you,' warned Davidson.

The other gave a hoarse laugh.

'What does it matter?' he said. 'You've got me for killing Lamont. I might as well admit to the others. There's one thing in my favour, you can only hang me once.' He looked across at Quest. 'Give me a cigarette and I'll tell you the whole story,' he said.

Silently the detective held out his case. Souza helped himself, struck a match, and after puffing for a moment or two at the cigarette began one of the most curious stories it had ever been Philip Quest's lot to listen to.

★   ★   ★

'There's no need for me to go over all the diamond stealing business again,' he said. 'I told that to Harding when he came out to Jo'burg making enquiries about Francis Lamont, and I've no doubt he's passed it on.'

He paused to look enquiringly at Quest, and the detective nodded.

'That was perfectly true, every word of it,' Souza continued. 'There was no reason why I shouldn't tell the truth then — because I wasn't mixed up in it any way. I only kept one thing back, and that was this: Lamont never took those diamonds out of South Africa. He knew he couldn't. He was under very strong suspicion of being mixed up in the robbery — a suspicion that was almost a certainty, and he knew that his luggage and himself would be searched at the port — as it was.

'So when he arrived in England he arrived without the diamonds. But he'd cached them somewhere out there in a place that was only known to himself. The original hiding place which Cowley, Bishop and Lamont had agreed upon he changed as soon as they were arrested. But I'll come to that later. Cowley had a sister of whom he was passionately fond. He used to talk to me a lot about her before the trouble. She was consumptive, and Cowley used to look after her — well, almost like a mother. She was much younger than he was — nearly ten years.

'When the trouble came and Cowley was arrested he was bothering more about his sister and what would happen to her than about himself. He told me about this a short while ago — not at the time it happened.

'He had often discussed with Bishop and Lamont what would happen to his sister if the diamond robbery should ever be discovered, and it was mutually arranged among them that whoever was caught — if any of them were — that the other or others should look after Mavis Cowley — that was his sister's name. That's why they, neither of them, gave Lamont away at the time.'

Manuel Souza paused and flicked a long cylinder of ash on the floor.

'I'm telling this rather badly, I'm afraid,' he said, 'but I must get this preliminary over. The part you are interested in comes later.'

Nobody said anything and he went on.

'Well, Lamont betrayed his trust and worse. As soon as Cowley and Bishop were safely in prison he cleared off — after removing the diamonds as I told you — and left Mavis Cowley to look after herself as best she could. Her best wasn't very good, and six months after she died, partly from consumption but mostly from starvation.

'During this time I was attending to my duties at the mine, and had almost forgotten the existence of the diamonds. I

271

should probably have forgotten them altogether if I hadn't run up against Cowley one night. He had escaped from the Breakwater and had come to look for his sister. He told me that Bishop was dead, and when I told him that Mavis was, too, he almost went mad. He swore that he would never rest until he had got even with Lamont for his treachery. And then he made his offer. If I could help him get away he would give me half share in the diamonds.

'The offer was a tempting one, for no one knew better than I the value of those stolen stones. I agreed, and he took me to the place on the veldt where the stones had been buried. We found the place all right, but that was all we did find. The diamonds had gone. Lamont had evidently moved them to some other hiding place. I knew he hadn't taken them out of the country because of the rigid search that he had undergone. Wherever they were hidden it was somewhere in the country, but we hadn't the faintest idea where. Cowley was all for going to England and finding Lamont, but the people from the Breakwater at Cape Town were looking for him, and I pointed out that it would be madness to attempt it. I suggested that he should lie concealed in a place I knew until the hue and cry had subsided, and he eventually agreed.

'The next thing we heard was that Lamont had committed suicide. I read an account of it in the paper, and told Cowley. He was furious that the man had succeeded in escaping his vengeance, but what worried me was the fact that all chance of ever finding the diamonds seemed gone for ever.

'I remembered, however, that Lamont had left a son and a daughter, and I wondered if he had confided in either of them before he died. My leave was not due for some time, and I didn't want to draw attention to myself by resigning my job, besides which I might never find the diamonds, in which case my job was all I had to live on. I decided, however, that when I got to England I would seek out the Lamonts and find out if their father had said anything about the diamonds.

'About this time Mr. Harding came out and began asking about Lamont. I told an abridged version of the affair, and he went away apparently quite satisfied.

'There is no need for me to go into details regarding what happened in the interval between Harding's visit and our — Cowley's and mine — arrival in England, because nothing happened. We just waited as patiently as we could. When we got to England the first thing I did was to seek out a man I knew whom I felt would be willing, for a small share of the diamonds, to help us. His name was Rule, and I had met him when he was visiting South Africa. I knew he was a drunken, unscrupulous sort of man, just the type I wanted. Rule was interested in the story I told him, and suggested that Merrick might be useful. I had already worked out the basis of a scheme, and the first thing I wanted to do was to find Harding.

'I discovered that he was living in Sydenham, and I went there, too, taking up my abode at the West Hill Hotel under the name of Ladlor.

'In my real capacity of Souza I called

on Harding, and from him I got the address of the Lamonts. I also learned that they were not still living in the house in which Francis Lamont had died, and that this was still empty. This information gave me an idea. It had been my original intention to go and see the Lamonts myself, but now I decided that I would send Cowley, and so make certain that there should be nothing to connect me with the Lamonts. I could always swear afterwards that although I had intended visiting them I had been prevented.

'I got Harding to write down the address of the Lamonts, and then asked him if I could borrow his car. He agreed, and I went off to find Cowley. To him I suggested my plan. He was to take the car, call on the Lamonts and ask for the son. He was to say that certain things had come to light concerning his father, the secret of which lay in an empty house in the safe concealed behind the seventh brick in the fireplace in Lamont's study.

'Of course, this was all nonsense, but he was to make it sound convincing enough to get Richard Lamont to accompany him to the empty house in Elm Tree Avenue where I would be waiting. It had been pretty foggy all day, but towards the evening it got so thick that you could scarcely see a yard before you, and this for us was an asset. Cowley went off to put his share of the scheme into execution, and I made my way to the empty house to await his arrival. He was a longer time coming than I expected, but eventually he arrived and Lamont with him.

'I met them at the door, to young Lamont's surprise, for he had not been told to expect a third person. However, I explained that Cowley was merely acting on my behalf, and that I was the principal person concerned. I said that I was representing De Greers Diamond Company, and that we believed that information concerning a quantity of diamonds that his father had stolen from the company was to be found in his concealed safe. I added that I acted in the way I had because I did not want there to be any scandal. He was, I could see, very surprised at my story. Obviously he had never heard anything about the diamonds, or that his father had been suspected of being concerned in their theft. But he was more surprised about the safe, assuring me that he believed I must be mistaken, and that he had never heard of its existence.

'I suggested that we should go and look for it and he agreed. Leaving Cowley outside with the car, we entered the house. Lamont wanted to go at once to the study, but since I knew there was nothing there I suggested that if he came in to one of the lower rooms I had something of importance to tell him first.

'When I got him inside I told him the complete story of the diamonds, and asked him if his father, before he died, had said anything that was likely to provide a clue to their whereabouts. He replied that he had given his sister two veils which he had told her to always keep in her possession, but had certainly given no explanation as to what they were for.

'You can imagine my excitement at this news. I was convinced that those veils held the secret of the place where Lamont had put the diamonds. I suggested that we should find his sister and get her to give us those veils, but something seemed to have aroused Lamont's suspicions, and he refused point blank. He said he wouldn't do anything further until he had consulted his lawyer, and said that I should arrange to accompany him on the following day.

'This would have meant disaster to all my plans. The whole thing would have come out. I tried to plead with him on the grounds of the scandal. His lawyer was a sensible man, and the whole thing could be done without any publicity at all. I lost my temper and threatened him, and then he said that he believed the whole story was a tissue of lies, and that he would inform the police and risk the scandal.

'I had a knife in my pocket which I always carried, and seeing that if he left the house alive the whole of my plans would be ruined, I stabbed him. He fell with scarcely a sound, and at that moment. I heard the sound of a car stopping somewhere outside. In a panic I hurried out of the house and joined Cowley. Hastily I told him what had happened and he was horrified. He said that he was going to have no hand in murder, and that he was finished with the whole matter. I told him that he was just as much involved as I was, and not to be a fool, and then we heard the sound of footsteps coming up the drive.

'I dragged Cowley into the shrubbery and we waited to see who was coming. Of course, it was Dr. Harman, and as you know the rest of what happened after there's no need for me to tell you.

'While he was inside the house Cowley and I slipped away. I arranged to meet him later in Elm Tree Avenue and went off to find Merrick. I found him where I usually met him in a little coffee shop off the High Street. I told him what had happened and sent him off to the Lamonts' house to secure the veils, and then I made my way back to the empty house in Elm Tree Avenue. I wanted to learn if possible, what was happening. I succeeded in creeping up the drive without being seen, and discovered that the police were already on the scene, and I was just going away again when I ran into a girl. She screamed, but I silenced her and took to my heels.

'For a long time I wandered about in the fog thinking. The police would, of course, find the car, and probably trace it to Harding, and Harding would say that he had lent it to me. I felt that I was in a nasty position, but I could think of no way out except that they would not believe Harding's story, and might suspect him of the crime. Anyhow, it would be difficult to trace me because I hadn't told any of them where I was living, and my name at the hotel was Ladlor, as I have said.

'I had come to no solution when the time for meeting Cowley came round. And here I got another shock. Cowley had been thinking things over, and he was scared. He repeated that he wasn't going to be mixed up with murder. The diamonds were a different matter. He felt that they were his by rights, but I had killed an innocent man and he wasn't going to stand for it. He was going to tell all he knew to the police. I could tell he meant what he said, although it would probably mean that he would have to go back to the Breakwater. I told him to do what he liked, and as he turned to leave me I stabbed him!

'I dragged his body into the garden of an adjacent house, and searched it to make sure there was nothing that would incriminate me. And then I had an idea. In my pocket was a card that Harding had given me and an old envelope with my name in which Cowley had delivered a note to me when we first came to England. If that envelope was found in Cowley's pocket the police might be led to believe that he was Souza. The only risk was that Harding might be asked to identify the body. I put the card in his hand with the object of further muddling the trail and throwing suspicion on Harding. If he was suspected his word wouldn't be taken for granted by the police, and they might easily think that the whole story of my calling and his loaning the car was a fabrication.

'I think that's all. When I called on Merrick that night and learned that he had not found the veils, I decided on the kidnapping of the girl. What happened you know, with the exception of this. I killed Merrick because he tried to blackmail me.'

Souza finished speaking, and for a moment there was silence. It was broken at last by Philip Quest.

'What is the secret of the veils?' he asked.

Souza shook his head.

'Except that I'm certain that they show where Lamont put those diamonds,' he replied, 'I don't know any more than you.'

23

The Secret of The Veils

Philip Quest was back in his office, and before him lay the two veils that Francis Lamont had given to his daughter before he died. They lay spread out on the desk, and over them bent Quest, a frown on his brow and a lens in his hands.

For hours after his return from Sydenham he had sat there trying with every atom of concentration of which he was capable to extract the secret that lay hidden among those folds of flimsy silk.

Lester, silently curled up in a corner of the big settee, watched him as he studied the veils for the thousandth time. The black marks of the embroidery conformed to no pattern, but were spread about haphazardly all over the fine surface. Again and again Quest had tried to resolve the marks into some kind of coherent design, but without result. They obstinately remained just a collection of black lines.

He examined the holes with their buttonhole stitching at each corner. They had obviously been made so that the veils could hang on something, but the question was what?

The afternoon was well advanced when he rose with a weary sigh.

'No luck?' enquired Lester sympathetically, and Quest shook his head irritably.

'No, I can't make any sense out of the things,' he answered. 'If they do contain a clue to the hiding place of those diamonds it's so well hidden that I don't think we shall ever find it.'

He lighted a cigarette, and began to walk up and down, his hands clasped behind him and his chin sunk on his breast.

Lester sighed hopelessly. He knew Quest in this mood. There would be no rest for the detective until he found out the secret that those veils contained. He would neither sleep nor eat; do nothing in fact until he had found a solution.

Tea was brought, but it was only Lester

who had any. Quest continued his ceaseless patrol of the room, his brows drawn together, only pausing to re-light a fresh cigarette from the box on the mantelpiece.

Lester had picked up a book and was trying to interest himself in its pages when a sudden exclamation from Quest made him look up. The detective had stopped suddenly in his pacing, and was standing stock still, his eyes gleaming.

'What is it?' asked the young man.

'Go and get the car out!' snapped Quest, 'and bring it round here as quickly as you can.'

Lester rose, opening his mouth to say something further; but Quest had already disappeared in his bedroom. With a shrug of his shoulders he struggled into his overcoat and hurried round to the garage. When he came back with the car he found Quest already waiting for him on the front steps.

Hurrying across the strip of pavement he got in beside Lester.

'Where to?' asked the young man.

'Sydenham!' answered Quest. 'The police

station, and drive as quickly as you can.'

Lester took these instructions literally, and he must have broken all records, for in a miraculously short time he drew up under the now familiar blue lamp.

'Wait here,' said Quest, as the car stopped. 'I shan't be a minute.'

He got out and hurried into the charge room. The desk sergeant looked up in surprise.

'Hello, sir!' he greeted. 'You are back again soon.'

'Is Inspector Davidson about?' asked Quest quickly.

'In his office, sir,' said the man, but Davidson must have heard the detective's voice, for as Quest took a step towards the door of his room he came out.

'Hello — ' he began, but Quest cut him short.

'Have you got the key of the house in Elm Tree Avenue?' he asked.

Davidson nodded.

'Let me have it, will you?' went on Quest quickly.

'What's the idea?' said Davidson curiously.

'I just want to test a theory of mine,' explained the detective. 'You can come along with me if you like.'

'Right, I will,' said the stout Inspector. 'I'll get the key.'

He disappeared into his office, and was back again almost at once. Quest led the way out to Lester and the waiting car.

'Elm Tree Avenue,' he ordered shortly, and got into the back with the Inspector.

'What's the idea?' asked Davidson again as the car started.

'You'll see when we get there,' replied Quest. 'But I think I'm going to show you the meaning of those veils.'

The house was very gloomy and forbidding as they drove up the drive. The windows stared silently into the night with a blank dead look. Davidson suppressed a shudder as they mounted the steps to the front door. He remembered the first occasion on which he had come to this dark and uninhabited place, and what he had found there.

Philip Quest drew out a powerful electric lamp while the Inspector opened the door, and switched it on as they passed into the passage.

'This way,' he said, when the three of them were inside and Davidson had closed the door. He began to ascend the stairs and, reaching the first landing stopped before a door on the right.

'This, if I remember the layout of the house as told me by Celia Lamont, should be Francis Lamont's study,' he said, and opened the door.

They entered a large bare room, dirty and musty-smelling. The floor was thick with dust and the paper had in places come away from the walls and hung in damp strips. Quest, after a quick glance round, went over to the two windows that overlooked the back garden. His light played round the frames, and he uttered a little exclamation of satisfaction.

'Look here, Lester — look at these, Davidson!' he called.

They came to his side quickly and he pointed to the frame of one of the windows. At each of the four corners of the lower sash had been screwed a small hook.

'Well, what about it?' demanded

Davidson. 'I can't see anything to get excited about. They've certainly been put there to hold a curtain — '

'Then look at these scratches on the glass itself,' interrupted Quest. 'Can you tell me what they are there for?'

The Inspector wrinkled his brows.

The lower pane was covered with a confusion of small scratches and curves which looked as though they had been made with a diamond.

'No, I can't,' he replied, shaking his head.

'Then I'll show you,' retorted Quest.

He took from his pocket an envelope, and extracting the two veils he hung them on the hooks, one over the other so that they covered the whole of the lower half of the window. When he had hung them to his satisfaction he bent forward and peered closely at the result.

'Now do you see?' he cried triumphantly. 'Shorthand! The markings on the veils and the scratchings on the window combine to form a message in shorthand. We can't read all of it tonight because it's dark outside, but if we come here first thing in the morning, with the daylight streaming through, I think you will find there where Lamont hid those diamonds!'

★   ★   ★

They did. It was clearly written in shorthand, and the reason that Lamont had gone to such trouble, was also obvious, for the place — out on the veldt in South Africa — required such minute directions for finding that no man could have trusted his memory.

'Where he got the veils made we shall never know,' remarked Quest, in answer to a question of Lester's. 'I've no doubt that if we visited all the people who do embroidery work in London we might eventually find out, but it isn't worth the trouble. He must have drawn what he wanted and had it copied. The markings on the window, of course, he could do himself, and the drawings from which the veils were made could have been done on transparent paper. It was a clever idea, because nobody could connect those veils with a written description of the hiding

290

place of the diamonds.'

De Greers were communicated with, and so the case, as far as Quest was concerned, was forgotten. Manuel Souza stood his trial, was found guilty and executed, and the last echo to reach the detective arrived at his city office one morning in the form of a registered packet.

It contained a beautiful stone that glittered and glistened in the morning sun, flashing a myriad colours across the breakfast table. Inside the wrapping was a card, 'With the compliments of De Greers, Ltd.'

THE END

We do hope that you have enjoyed reading this large print book.

Did you know that all of our titles are available for purchase?

We publish a wide range of high quality large print books including:
Romances, Mysteries, Classics
General Fiction
Non Fiction and Westerns

Special interest titles available in large print are:
The Little Oxford Dictionary
Music Book, Song Book
Hymn Book, Service Book

Also available from us courtesy of Oxford University Press:
Young Readers' Dictionary
(large print edition)
Young Readers' Thesaurus
(large print edition)

For further information or a free brochure, please contact us at:
Ulverscroft Large Print Books Ltd.,
The Green, Bradgate Road, Anstey,
Leicester, LE7 7FU, England.
Tel: (00 44) **0116 236 4325**
Fax: (00 44) **0116 234 0205**

S.T.A.R. FLIGHT

E. C. Tubb

The Kaltich invaders are cruelly prolonging their Earthmen serfs' lives and denying them the secret of instantaneous space travel, so desperately needed by a barbaric, overpopulated Earth. While the Kaltichs strip Earth of its riches, the Secret Terran Armed Resistance movement, STAR, opposes them — but it's only their agent, Martin Preston, who can possibly steal the aliens' secrets. If he fails, billions of people will starve — with no place to go to except to their graves.

THE SILENT WORLD

John Russell Fearn

Around the world there was total silence from Pole to Pole. Seas crashed noiselessly on rocky shores, hurricanes shrieked mutely across the China Sea. People shouted and were not heard; alarms and bells rang and yet were mute. The dead wall of silence was everywhere — the most strident sound was unable to break through it. Scientists were unprepared for The Silence. There was something amiss with the laws which governed sound — but that was only the beginning . . .

DOUBLE ILLUSION

Philip E. High

Earth — four hundred years from now — a rotten society in which mankind is doomed to die out — and one seemingly average man with incredible I.Q. potential . . . An ultra-intelligent computer is built and used to govern humanity — and all corruption in the world is eradicated. Mother Machine decides what's best for her human children — and it is done. But the all-powerful computer is turning mankind into zombies. The world's only hope lies in one outlawed, not-so-average man . . .

A WOMAN TO DIE FOR

Steve Hayes

When hard-nosed PI Mitch Holliday loses his licence, he helps his partner, Lionel Banks, to pick up a missing girl named Lila Hendricks. But everything goes wrong; Mitch is drawn into a world of money, murder and double-cross. Seduced by socialite Claire Dixon's wealth — murder is now the name of the game. The target is a wealthy businessman with few redeeming qualities. Would Mitch, tough and cynical as he is, kill for the promise of love and money?

MEET JIMMY STRANGE

Ernest Dudley

Jimmy Strange was a mysterious young man who'd turn up when he was least expected; wherever there was trouble, he'd appear from behind some dark corner. No one knew much about him, though he was always a gentleman. He was never short of money, but where it came from no one knew. He wasn't a crook — yet they did say he could break into a house with the best of them — but always in a good cause . . .

SIX STRANGE CASES

Rafe McGregor

Private investigator Titus Farrow is doomed by an encounter with the Chambers Scroll; Roderick Langham solves the mystery of the 'Demeter' from his armchair by the sea; a failed author goes in search of the barghest for inspiration; a missing person case turns even nastier than blackmail; Sweeney Todd meets his match . . . These stories make a gripping journey through 'The King in Yellow', 'Dracula', 'Sweeney Todd', and the noir fiction of the pulp era.